THE HOLLYWOOD **BOOK SEVENTEEN** MURDER MYSTERIES
1963

# CUE THE CROWS

D1484297

# PETER S. FISCHER

www.petersfischer.com

ALSO BY PETER S. FISCHER

*Me and Murder, She Wrote*
*Expendable: A Tale of Love and War*
*The Blood of Tyrants*
*The Terror of Tyrants*

**The Hollywood Murder Mystery Series**

*Jezebel in Blue Satin*
*We Don't Need No Stinking Badges*
*Love Has Nothing to Do With It*
*Everybody Wants An Oscar*
*The Unkindness of Strangers*
*Nice Guys Finish Dead*
*Pray For Us Sinners*
*Has Anybody Here Seen Wyckham?*
*Eyewitness to Murder*
*A Deadly Shoot in Texas*
*Everybody Let's Rock*
*A Touch of Homicide*
*Some Like 'Em Dead*
*Dead Men Pay No Debts*
*Apple Annie and the Dude*
*Till Death Us Do Part*
*Cue the Crows*

ISBN 978-0-9960491-6-0

*To my loving wife Lucille,*
*may she frolic with the angels.*
*59 years of ups and downs*
*and I loved every minute of it.*

# CHAPTER ONE

Vacation. And it's about time.

That's the way Bunny put it. She's been hounding me for weeks to cut loose for a family holiday. Either that or start another book because I have been grouching around the house (her words) for far too long and Joe Bernardi at loose ends with nothing to occupy his time is not a Joe Bernardi anyone wants to deal with. Okay, so holiday time it is. My newest book, "Jezebel in Blue Satin" has been acquired by my publisher, Posieden Literary House, for summer release and in late June I'm going to have to start making the publicity rounds. But this is mid-May and June is a month away. A lot of these dates have already been inked in and I have about six grueling weeks of interviews and appearances to look forward to. My next book is nothing more than a germ of an idea and poses a bevy of plot problems. Another reason why my usual sunny disposition is not in evidence. Vacation? Sure. Good idea. Bunny has been given a week off from her job at the Valley News and the Amelia Ogilvy School for Young Ladies doesn't care if we abscond with my nine-year-old daughter Yvette for a week, provided her tuition is paid up. It is.

I also have another reason for embarking on this holiday, a reason unknown to Bunny and it's going to stay that way until the last possible moment.

Writing 'Jezebel' was both a labor of love and a joy and I will be forever grateful to Truman Capote and Harper Lee for shaking me loose from a lucrative but increasingly tedious sixteen-year career as a movie publicist to follow my dream. Oh, I have pitched in a few times with a publicity gig over the past year when my former partner, Bertha Bowles, has needed a hand. The least I could do for old times sake, particularly when our company, still called Bowles & Bernardi, sends me a healthy check each month out of the profits. But make no mistake, as I told Bertha, I am an author now and I'm going to stay one.

My seldom-reliable but beautiful and comfortable Bentley is cruising easily north on the Pacific Coast Highway while Bunny and Yvette take in the gorgeous scenery. I get a lot of "Hey, Daddy, look!"s from Yvette which I ignore lest I put the car into the ocean or a roadside barranca. Sightseeing is not for drivers, not on the PCH, not with its treacherous curves, especially near Big Sur. Just north of Monterey, we cut across to the 101 which is a straight shot into the heart of San Francisco where we are booked into a suite at the St. Francis for two nights. Two days is more than enough to take in the sights, the sounds and the smells of this unique city with its Embarcadero, Fisherman's Wharf, the Presidio, Chinatown, and its vibrant theater district. Tonight we have reservations at The Old Clam House. Tomorrow, Mother's Day, Bunny calls the shots and even though she isn't technically Yvette's mother, she's close enough for the both of us.

Two days pass quickly. The city doesn't disappoint and Yvette drinks it in like a thirsty Bedouin who has just come upon an oasis. Like her birth mother Jillian Marx, my daughter is fearless and adventurous, opting for eel instead of hamburger and octopus instead of fried chicken. I almost dread the teen years when she will start to explore the world around her, i.e. boys. Bunny tells me not to worry. Yvette has a head on her shoulders. She'll be just fine.

I wish I could share her certainty. Then I remember that Jill, with whom I had had a brief fling, was no fool. I feel better but not much.

And now it's Tuesday morning. The valet brings the car around and we head for the Golden Gate Bridge and points north. When we reach the end of the bridge I turn off and continue north on Rte 1. Bunny, like the late Jillian Marx, is also no fool.

"I thought we were going to explore the wine country," she says, giving me the fisheye.

"We are," I assure her.

"Then why are we going up the coast? We should be heading inland toward Napa."

Busted.

"It's a little out of our way but there's someone I have to see a few miles up the road."

"Aha!" she says triumphantly.

"Aha what?"

"Aha," she repeats herself.

"It won't take long. I didn't mention it until now because I was sure you'd get the wrong idea."

"A favor for Bertha," she says knowingly.

"Sort of."

"Sort of what?"

I squirm a little. I'm leery about telling her. My screenplay has become something of a joke between us, even though it is a very good screenplay and Bunny loves it and it's based on my acclaimed first novel which I wrote several years ago. But every year it seems somebody wants to make the picture and everything goes along well until the last minute and then the bottom falls out. The money's not there, the star dropped out, the foreign rights can't be sold. It's always something, yet, here we go again.

"There's a location shoot just north of here at Bodega Bay. I need to pay a courtesy call on one of our new clients. Tippi Hedren."

"Our new clients? You are retired, Joe, or have you forgotten?"

"I still have ties to the company, Bunny."

"Yeah. Well, let somebody else make the courtesy calls." She stops and out of the corner of my eye I can see her staring at me. "Or is there something else?"

"What could there be?"

"Joe?" she insists.

Damn. To Bunny I am an open book. Don't know why. I just am.

"The screenplay. It's been optioned." I tell her.

"What? Again?"

"I think this may be it, Bunny. Two young hotshots named Jerry Kaplan and Pat Brady have broken away from Paramount to form their own production company. They love the screenplay."

"Who doesn't?" Bunny says. "They all love it but it never gets made."

"This'll be different. They've got money and contacts and Paul Wendkos has indicated he wants to direct it."

"What happened to Stu Rosenberg?"

"Unavailable. Developing some kind of chain gang picture for Paul Newman."

"Lah-de-dah. And who's this guy Wendkos? Never heard of him."

"Last year he directed a picture called Angel Baby about evangelism. Reviews were so-so but the guy got raves. He has talent and we can afford him."

"What's this 'we' business, sport?"

"I mean, they."

"Good thing," Bunny says irritably. "Like you told me, lover, only idiots invest in Broadway or the movies."

"Absolutely," I reply, not telling her that I have agreed to forego any compensation, settling instead for a piece of the profits.

"Don't fight, please. I'm trying to color," comes a voice from the back seat. I check my rear view. Yvette has her tongue out, concentrating mightily on her Elvis Presley coloring book.

"We're not fighting, honey," I say. "Just discussing."

"Maybe you could discuss more quietly," Yvette says.

My daughter. Nine, going on thirty.

Bunny shakes her head.

"I'm not sure I can take it again, Joe. You getting your hopes up and then it all falls apart. Last time almost killed you."

"Like I said, Bunny, this one's different."

"Okay, so we meet Mr. Wendkos and make nice and what else?"

"Well, actually, this picture, Wendkos isn't directing it. Hitch is."

"Hitch? You mean Hitchcock?"

"Yes."

"I think I read a release about this. Something about birds."

"Right."

"Crazy birds who try to kill people."

"Something like that."

"Well, if we're not going to see Wendkos, what are we going for? Besides Tippi."

"I need to soft soap an actor."

"Oh,no, I hate actors," Bunny grouses.

"He'll be perfect to play Walt."

"You talk to him. I'll hang out on the beach with Yvette. What's this guy's name?"

"Rod Taylor."

Bunny looks at me sharply, almost in disbelief.

"Rod Taylor? Two years ago he turned you down."

"No, he had another commitment he couldn't get out of."

"Same thing," she says, crossing her arms and staring at the scenery racing by.

"It is not the same thing," I tell her. "Anyway, his TV series is done with and he has nothing until later in the year and he loves the script and he loves the part and if Jerry and Pat can make the money and the billing work, he's ours. Unless of course, you don't like him."

"Of course, I like him. I like him a lot."

I shake my head. "Even though he's not your type."

"Who said that?"

"You did. Two years ago."

"Oh? Well, I was annoyed." Then with a beady look "And what's my type supposed to be?"

"Me," I reply with a grin.

"Hah!" she says turning her attention back to the scenery.

Twenty minutes later I spot the sign "Bodega Bay 1 Mile" and the traffic slows to a crawl. We edge forward until we reach a highway patrolman who is shunting everyone off onto a detour. I roll down my window.

"What's going on, Officer?" I ask, already able to guess the answer.

"Traffic's detouring around the town, sir. They're shooting a movie."

"Yes, I know. Mr. Hitchcock is a friend of mine."

"Is he expecting you?"

"No, but he'll be delighted to see me. We go back a long way." I hand him my card and then pull out of line to the side of the road while he walkie-talkies my particulars to the set. Five minutes later he signals me back onto the road and points straight ahead.

"Go slow, Mr. Bernardi, and watch for the flagman. If he waves you to a stop, pull over. It means the camera will be rolling."

"I know the drill, Officer, and thank you."

I pull ahead slowly and a couple of minutes later I spot the security guard with his red flag sitting on a camp chair. He gets up and intercepts me. Well over six feet tall and obviously well-muscled, he could pass for Jim Arness's brother. His name tag reads 'Waldo'.

"Straight ahead, Mr. Bernardi. Take a left onto Harbor Way to the end. Heron Drive. That's where you'll find the trucks. Park there and one of the Teamsters will ferry you over to where they are shooting."

I thank him and follow instructions. At Heron Drive I find a dozen trucks including the caterer who is putting out the tables and chairs for the lunch break. A beefy grey-haired guy wearing a black windbreaker with "The Birds" silk-screened on the back approaches, hand extended, as I get out of the car.

"Mr. Bernardi? Moe Byrnes. I'm going to drive you to the set." He peers into the car and smiles at Bunny. "Morning, ma'am." His eyes fall on Yvette and he frowns imperceptibly. "Maybe the little one would rather stay here. I'm sure Manny could rustle up some ice cream or a soda." It's his way of saying that a nine year old would just be in the way and he might be right.

"Yvette, would you like to come to the set and watch them film the movie?"

"Boring," she says flatly without looking up. And she's right, of course. Watching a movie being filmed is akin to watching ice melt but less fun, and she's been there, done that. I leave her in the care of Manny, the caterer, who has dug up some chocolate ice cream and as we head for the harbor, I look back and Yvette has settled in at one of the plank tables, spooning ice cream with one hand and coloring Elvis with the other. Along with everything else, ambidextrous.

Several minutes later we arrive at the set which is extensive. The centerpiece appears to be a restaurant called the Tides Wharf with a gas station nearby, cars parked everywhere, some new and most not. At first glance it appears that not much is going on. A young woman in a khaki pants suit and a couple of cameras hanging around her neck is flitting about, capturing the work in progress. Now I spot gaffers setting lights and positioning reflectors while

Robert Burks, the Director of Photography, looks on. The camera is set back and unless it's repositioned, the first shot will be wide and all-encompassing. I know Bob from the shoot in Quebec City where Hitch was directing 'I Confess'. Bob hasn't changed much in nine years and I guess I haven't either because when I catch his eye, he smiles and waves a greeting. I wave back. That's when I spot Hitch sitting at a table on the outskirts of the set, his portly frame shaded by an umbrella. He seems to be in a crisis conference with someone I don't recognize.

"I'm going to say hi to Hitch. You want to join me?" I say.

"I'll be right there. I'm going to grab a cup of coffee from craft services," Bunny replies heading toward the goodie table set up across the way. I watch her go, then amble over to Hitchcock. He looks up as I approach and smiles.

"Joseph, delighted to see you. Come, come, sit. Say hello to Peggy Robertson, my good right arm, next to Alma, of course." Alma's his wife, a former editor and his principal sounding board.

Peggy and I greet each other as I pull up a chair.

"Good to see you, too, Hitch. Been far too long."

"It most certainly has," he agrees.

I point to the activity.

"What's the setup?" I ask.

"Exciting. Most exciting. The wharf is about to be attacked by a gang of murderous birds. People run, they scream, gasoline accidentally floods the wharf, a careless match and whoosh, everything is aflame as the birds continue to attack."

"Sounds great. Where's the local fire brigade?"

"Unneeded. This shot will be establishing, pre-calamity. The fireworks will be shot back at Universal where I will have more control. Odd about these birds, Joseph. They have great difficulty taking direction. Worse than actors."

I grin. "They haven't yet learned who they are dealing with."

He grins back. "You jest but with a soupcon of truth, old friend. Peggy and I were just discussing the positioning of my cameo appearance and I have decided on earlier rather than later. In fact it's to be the first scene, me with two hounds on leashes exiting a pet store."

"Cute," I say.

"More than cute, Joseph. A necessity. I am convinced that my loyal fans spend an inordinate amount of time looking for that special moment when I appear, detracting from their attention to the film. Therefore, we get it out of the way and get on with the suspense, terror and whatever mayhem is in store."

Peggy rises from her chair. "I'll notify Norman about the opening scene, Mr. Hitchcock. Nice to meet you, Mr. Bernardi."

"My pleasure, Ms. Robertson," I smile as she bustles away.

"So, Joseph," Hitchcock says, "may I assume you have come to your senses and submitted to Universal's imprecations to publicize this marvelous film in the making which will most certainly be a gemstone in my ouevre."

"You mean, have I returned to the wonderful world of flackery? Most assuredly not, Hitch. I am now a bona fide novelist and I intend to stay that way."

"Yes, Alma read your new book, the murder mystery, and loved it. Says it may be something for me."

"I'd be flattered," I say.

"You've also become something of a screenwriter," Hitchcock says. "Have I heard correctly that the two young Turks who fled Paramount are ready to film your first novel?"

"They are," I say, "which is the reason I have dropped by, in addition to renewing old acquaintance with a dear friend, of course."

Hitchcock smiles knowingly. "Then you've obviously come to wine and dine Mr. Taylor. Yes, Joseph, I did read your screenplay and it is excellent and Mr. Taylor, well directed, will make an excellent Walt. But of course that's true of all actors, they must be well directed or if not, of what use are they, the poor things." He looks past me. "Oh, dear," he says, "it appears your wife has already begun the wining and the dining or at least the equivalent thereof."

I turn in my chair to see Bunny at the crafts services table, coffee mug in hand, standing so close to Rod Taylor you couldn't slip the ace of spades between them and smiling up into his ruddy Aussie face.

"That is your wife, I presume, Joseph," Hitchcock says with a twinkle.

I nod and stand up.

"Excuse me, Hitch, but I think I'd better go remind her of that fact. Catch you later."

"Indeed," he says, turning his attention back to his open script. Just then the shutterbug in khaki approaches, camera at the ready.

"Mr. Hitchcock?"

He looks up, then smiles as she rips off three quick shots.

"Thanks," she says as she smiles at me, then hurries off to immortalize a few of the hard working crew members.

"Gracie something-or-other. With the Santa Rosa paper," Hitch explains. "Any publicity is good publicity, am I right, Joe?"

"Absolutely, Hitch," I say as I turn and head for the craft services table.

Bunny has her back to me but Taylor sees me coming and extricates himself adroitly as I approach. He smiles warmly, hand extended.

"Mr. Bernardi, a real pleasure to finally meet you."

His grip is firm and I see warmth and sincerity in his eyes.

"I echo the sentiment, Mr. Taylor," I say returning warmth and sincerity in equal measure.

"That's Rod," he says.

"Joe," I say.

"Bunny," she says, lightly holding Taylor's arm.

"Your biggest fan," Rod says, glancing at Bunny, "but you already know that. She absolutely insists that I do your film. Says I'd be perfect."

"I agree," I say.

"So do I," Rod says. "And as soon as your people and my people finish quibbling about the paperwork, I'm yours."

"Good to hear," I say. "How are you and Hitch getting along?"

"Fine. He's a charming tyrant, but then, you already know that. The girl isn't faring quite as well."

"The girl?"

"Tippi. Tippi Hedren. That's what he calls her. The girl. She's new at this but he's not giving her much wiggle room."

I shrug. "Hitch has his quirks," I say.

"Mmm," Rod says, "and one is the obligatory blonde. I think he had his heart set on Grace Kelly and Cary Grant. Grace up and married her prince but I have no idea why Cary passed. Anyway I'm used to being second or third choice."

"Not by me, you're not," I tell him.

"Thanks for saying it," he replies. "So what are your plans?"

"Nothing firm," Bunny pipes up. "We can stay all day."

"Sweet of you, Bunny," Taylor says, " but I'm going to be tied up. Look, why don't we have dinner this evening. I'm staying at the Bodega Bay Arms. It's close by and the food's excellent and we can get better acquainted while we discuss the movie."

"Well..." I start hesitantly.

"Wonderful idea," Bunny grins. "We'd be delighted, wouldn't we, Joe?"

Those sparkling, hopeful eyes. How can I resist them? And incidentally, I think to myself, what's this Australian hunk have that I don't?

Just then I hear a voice.

"Smile, folks." Gracie something-or-other has us in the sights of her 35 mm and we all smile in unison as she clicks off a couple of shots.

"Much obliged," she says, turning to look for new prey. I can see the photo caption now. 'International film star Rod Taylor chatting with fans on the set of Alfred Hitchcock's new film.' Gracie is very young and has a lot to learn about newspapering such as getting names to go with the photo. I may have a chat with her.

"So, what do you say, Joe?" Rod says. "Seven thirty? We'll be wrapped by then. And I think there's a good chance Mary might join us."

Bunny looks up at him sharply.

"Mary?"

"My fiancee. We're getting married on the first of June."

"Oh, how lovely," Bunny manages to say with a minimum of sincerity.

"She's up to her ears in wedding arrangements but she's going to try for the four-thirty flight out of LAX."

Bunny smiles politely. I put my arm around her and give her a squeeze.

"Don't look so glum, sweetheart," I say, "you've always got me." I squeeze her harder. A lot harder. She gives me a look that says don't do that again. I decide not to.

# CHAPTER TWO

The Bodega Bay Arms Hotel, the largest and oldest hotel in Sonoma County, is unique. What was once an imposing Victorian home sitting on a bluff overlooking the bay is now a sprawling but welcoming rest stop for weary travelers. It has been added to over the years; a west wing, an east wing, a huge kitchen and dining room, an oak paneled bar, a plush reception area and outside, a swimming pool and tennis courts. Despite the obvious amenities, the parking lot is far from full. I wonder why.

A fresh faced young man grabs our luggage from the Bentley's boot while Bunny and Yvette and I traipse inside to register for the night. Dinner with Rod at seven-thirty until at least nine and then what? Go where? When the dowdy room clerk tells me we can have a large airy room with a king sized bed and a rollaway for Yvette, I'm sold. It's when I look at the room rate on the registration form that I realize why the place is not overflowing with guests. Crew members can find decent accommodations down on the highway at half the price. An octogenarian bellman loads our bags onto a trolley and we start for the elevator. I pass the bar, peer in and spot a familiar face sitting by himself. His eye catches mine and smiles. He waves. I turn to Bunny.

"You go up and get us settled. I just spotted an old friend," I say.

"What's her name?" she asks.

"I forget. She's wearing a six day five o'clock shadow."

"Good thing." This from a woman who was recently hanging all over Rod Taylor like tinsel on a Christmas tree. "If we're not in the room, look for us by the pool," she says.

"Right."

I walk into the bar. My old friend rises from his bar stool and steps forward to greet me, hand extended.

"Joe."

"Evan."

We shake and go back to the bar where I order a Coors. Evan's been imbibing something a little stronger. I first met Evan Hunter three years ago at a Writers Guild meeting, the two of us laughing privately at all the old lefties from the 30's screaming "Strike! Strike!" and then, as usual, doing nothing about it. We went out for drinks afterward and have kept in touch ever since.

"So, goombah, what are you doing here?" I ask.

"Working, paisan. How about you?" he replies.

Most people know that Evan Hunter publishes books under a half dozen aliases, most notably Ed McBain, but few are aware that he was born Salvatore Albert Lombino of Italian parentage in East Harlem thirty-seven years ago.

"What do you mean, working?" I ask.

"I mean, I'm the screenwriter of this opus, Joe. At least I think I am. This bar is my oasis but I spend most of the day in my motorhome trying to make sense out of Hitch's notes, some of which came straight from his so-called muse."

"Muse? Sorry. You lost me."

"Mr. Cronyn."

"Hume Cronyn?"

"The same. He's here with his wife Jessica Tandy who has a major part."

"Still don't get it," I say.

"Hitch has a fascination, mostly undeserved, of Cronyn's script savvy. Cronyn helped make a mishmosh of 'Under Capricorn'. Now he's trying to meddle the same way on this picture. It wouldn't be so bad but every morning Hitch and I get up with the sun and commute here by limo from the Fairmont in San Francisco. Hitch passes along Cronyn's ideas as if they were his own and I'm trapped. No escape for the weary."

Evan drains the rest of his drink and taps his glass on the bar for a refill. The bartender approaches.

"Doesn't sound like Hitch," I say.

"Well, it is but Cronyn's not the only problem. Hitch has some weird ideas of his own which no self-respecting writer would put up with. But then I'm not sure I'm self-respecting, Joe. What do you think?"

"If you're not, you should be," I say. "A lot of good stuff has come out of that prolific brain of yours and not just 'The Blackboard Jungle'."

"Thanks for that, Joe." The bartender brings his refill and he raises it to his lips. "Here's to us writers. Ignored, irrelevant and demeaned. But what would they do without us?"

I watch him down half the glass and wonder how he got to be so cynical since the last time I saw him.

Twenty minutes later, I'm entering our second floor room, still bothered by Evan's dour attitude. Obviously this is not the happiest of sets and while Rod was reluctant to really say so, Tippi Hedren, his vivacious blonde leading lady, is getting the brunt of Hitchcock's dissatisfaction. As Evan explains it, the first section of the movie is designed to be sophisticated screwball comedy, to lull the audience before the terror suddenly comes out of nowhere and won't go away. Written for Cary and Grace, it doesn't work all that well with Rod and Tippi. Rod is a terrific meat and potatoes "everyman", Evan says, but Cary Grant he is not. As for Tippi she's new at this and there is an obvious undercurrent of tension between her and Hitchcock. Whether it's entirely about her acting I have no idea but rumors have been flying for years about his obsession with blonde leading ladies. I think back to Canada where Hitch was filming "I Confess'. Anne Baxter, a lovely brunette in all her other films, oddly went blonde as Monty Clift's star-crossed lover.

I look out the window at the swimming pool across from the parking lot where Yvette is splashing about and even swimming now and then. Bunny is relaxing in a nearby chaise, reading a book. Our bags have been unpacked so I begin a search for my swim trunks.

At twenty past seven, showered and tastefully garbed, Bunny and I get ready to leave the room. Yvette is propped up on the bed, a room service tray in her lap: spaghetti, a hot dog, potato chips, and butter pecan ice cream. The TV set is tuned to 'The Flintstones'. We throw her a kiss. She hardly notices, transfixed by Fred and Barney Rubble. We leave and head for the dining room located on the main floor just off the reception area. Rod has yet to arrive but the table's been reserved and our waiter leads us to it. I order an iced coffee, Bunny, a recovering alcoholic with seven years sobriety, settles for orange juice and I start to tell her about my odd conversation with Evan Hunter. At that moment, something in the lobby catches my eye. Bunny turns to look.

Rod is in a heated conversation with a young woman and they are going toe to toe. I can't hear what's being said but they are definitely not exchanging best wishes. She's a redhead with longish hair and a body that won't quit but I can't pinpoint her age. She could be eighteen or twenty eight and I am pretty damned sure this is not his fiancee. At least I hope not. He pushes past her and heads for the reception desk where the clerk hands him the phone. She turns on her heel and hurries out the main entrance. He watches her go, then pushes the phone away and heads in our direction.

When he reaches the table, I smile up at him.

"Mary?"

"God, no," he says. "I need a drink."

Our waiter hurries over and takes his order for a double scotch. Rod pulls up his chair.

"Mary called. Can't make it. As for little Miss Red Head, that is a long and painful story. Some day when I have a week, I'll tell you about her."

"No fair," Bunny says. "I love long and painful stories."

Rod smiles.

"Okay, I'll give you the abridged version. She's a leech and I can't get rid of her. I took her out a couple of times early last year before I met Mary. Then I discovered she was only nineteen. She looked and acted like twenty-nine but by then she was becoming suffocating so I broke it off. I did. She didn't. Amanda—that's her name, Amanda Broome, a UCLA dropout—continued to chase me and I finally had to get a restraining order. The truth is she's unbalanced. No sense of reality. And she's driving me nuts. I thought up here I'd get a break but no, somehow she found out where I'd be and she just showed up. As you saw when I threatened to call the cops, she ran for it."

"Well, Amanda can't make Mary very happy," Bunny says as the waiter returns with Rod's drink and three menus and then hovers nearby, pencil at the ready.

"Mary's been great but her patience isn't limitless any more than mine is. Maybe we'll get lucky. Maybe she'll get run over by a truck."

I smile slyly. "I spotted a Ryder Rental outlet at the edge of town when we drove in."

He laughs. "Great. I'll give 'em a call first thing in the morning. Come on, let's order. I'm starved."

We order and I watch Rod carefully. Then as the waiter leaves for the kitchen, I say, "You know, Rod, there's more than a little Aussie in your speech."

"Oh, my mistake," he says innocently, looking around. "Is there a camera rolling?"

"None I know of," I say.

"So, Joe, are you a Dodger fan?" he asks.

"St. Louis Cards," I reply.

He nods. "Close enough. Maury Wills on second, Willie Davis on first and big Frank Howard striding to the plate. So far today the big fella's two for three with a two run homer in the third. Marichal looks in. Howard taps the plate. Marichal sets throws. Ball one, low and outside." Rod smiles. "Any questions?"

"None," I admit, a little chagrined. The gentleman from New South Wales has just done a perfect imitation of Vin Scully calling a Dodger game, as American as an Iowa farmboy. We chat amiably through dinner and share the latest gossip. He tells us about Mitch Zankich, the owner of the Tides restaurant who granted permission to film there with three provisos: the town would be called Bodega Bay, Rod's character would be named 'Mitch' and Zankich would get a speaking part in the film. I grin inwardly. Everybody wants to be in the movies. Finally we get around to the screenplay as well as the book which Rod has also read. I'm impressed. He has a flawless vision of the character of Walt, who he is and how he should be played. The more he talks the more I realize he is a perfect choice. Now if the lawyers and the bean counters would just get out of the way, we could proceed to make the damned picture.

By ten o'clock we're pretty much talked out. Three times I tried to bring Tippi Hedren into the conversation. In a weak moment he tells us that he is under orders from Hitchcock not to touch Tippi once he has called 'Cut!' on the set. When I ask him why such a ridiculous demand, Rod is either evasive or changes the subject. Something is going on and whatever it is is either a publicist's dream or a nightmare. Thank God it's no longer my business. Meanwhile Rod needs to get to bed. He has a ten a.m. call the next morning. I don't so I'm going to sleep in but I'll be up before noon checkout time. We shake, Bunny hugs, and we both tell him how much we are looking forward to making 'A Family of Strangers'. No, we can't stick around. We're headed for the Napa Valley but I promise him we'll stay in touch.

We find Yvette sprawled in bed, dead asleep, the television set still on. Bunny and I bundle her into the rollaway and get ready for sleep. I say sleep because with the kid a scant few feet away, hi jinx for the evening are definitely not on the agenda. Three straight days now without any Bunny-love. I'm getting peevish.

I'm awakened hours later by loud voices under my window. The clock on the night table reads ten past seven and the sun is rising in the east. I get up and look out at the scene below. Two squad cars marked 'Sonoma County Sheriff's Department' are parked close by. One's radio is squawking. A guy in uniform with three stripes on his sleeve is talking to Rod while a half dozen guests are nearby gawking at the scene. I don't like the sight or the sounds of it. That's my meal ticket the sergeant is jawing at. I throw on slacks, a shirt and sandals and hurry out the door leaving Bunny and Yvette fast asleep. Once downstairs I hurry out the front entrance to find Rod giving as good as he's getting.

"And I'm telling you, Sergeant, I don't know what the hell you're talking about," Rod is saying. "I turned in last night around ten thirty and slept the night away, awakened by your goon over there. It's obvious you have the wrong man or someone's playing a huge practical joke on you."

"If it's a joke, I find it very unfunny," the cop is saying.

Rod spots me."Here. Here's my friend, Mr. Bernardi. He and his wife were having dinner with me from half seven to well past ten o'clock."

The sergeant, whose name tag reads 'Hayes', looks at me briefly and then dismisses me, turning his attention back to Rod.

"And after ten thirty? Look, Mr. Taylor, we got a tip that someone had stuffed a body into the trunk of a white Corvette in the parking lot of the Bodega Bay Arms hotel sometime after midnight and yours is the only white Corvette on the premises."

"Tip? What kind of tip? From whom?"

"Anonymous."

"Anonymous. Wonderful. Man or woman?"

"Man, I think."

"Man, you think. Tell you what, Sergeant, tonight I'm going to call your office and anonymously report that a pot-bellied Sheriff's deputy with three stripes on his sleeve was seen raping a woman in back of a Chinese restaurant in Santa Rosa. How's that for an anonymous tip?"

"Maybe you find this amusing," Sergeant Hayes says, sucking in his gut. "I don't."

"Amusing? I find it ludicrous. Where's your warrant? Even in primitive Australia we know about warrants."

"I can get one."

"Can you? I wonder."

"I should warn you, Mr. Taylor, I have a witness who overheard you discussing running this woman down with a truck."

"Oh, for God's sake, that was a joke."

"Was it?"

"No," Rod says angrily, "I decided it was too much trouble to rent a truck so I switched to a baseball bat instead."

"Look, all I'm asking for is a little cooperation," Hayes says.

"And maybe if your brain dead underling over there hadn't pounded on my door and tried to drag me out of my room in handcuffs and my pajamas, I'd be inclined to give it."

Hayes throws a sideways glare at one of his men leaning idly against one of the squad cars. "I've already apologized for that."

Rod looks over at me. He's steaming. I shrug. He hesitates, then reaches on his pocket for his car keys and slaps them into the sergeant's hand. "Knock yourself out. The car's over there. Second row."

"Thank you," Hayes says icily as he turns and heads toward the car. Rod and I follow. Deftly Hayes inserts the key and then lifts the lid. As he does she comes into view. Red hair disheveled, slate grey eyes starting into nothingness, congealed blood turning from red to brown on her face and cheek, her neck has been sliced open from ear to ear.

"Jesus Christ," Rod gasps in disbelief.

Hayes stares at her for a moment.

"Do you know this woman, Mr. Taylor?" he asks.

"Yes," Rod manages to say, "but I don't know anything about this."

"These keys," the sergeant says holding them up, "is this the only set?"

"Yes."

"Have they been out of your sight?"

"No. I mean, not that I know of."

Hayes leans in for a closer look, then calls out to one of his men.

"Philby, radio headquarters. I want the forensic team out here right away."

"Yes, sir," one of the officers says, hurrying to one of the squad cars, as Hayes turns his attention back to Rod.

"You say you knew her."

"Her name was Amanda Broome."

"I'm going to need a statement."

"Yes," Rod says. "I need to call the production office and tell them what's happened. I'm supposed to be on the set by ten."

"I doubt that's going to happen," the sergeant says dryly. "Let's go inside. Sanchez, stay by the car. Close the trunk. Keep away the gawkers."

"Yes, sir."

Rod and the sergeant start inside. I tag along. If Hayes notices or objects, he gives no sign. We find a deserted corner of the dining room where breakfast is just being served. They sit down at a table. I sit down with them.

"This interview is private, sir," Hayes says.

I smile. "Joseph Bernardi. I'm his lawyer," I lie. "Bowles & Bernardi. Los Angeles. We're in the book." It's all Rod can do to keep from laughing out loud.

"How convenient," the sergeant says and then turns his attention back to Rod who tells him what he knows. Her name was Amanda Broome. An only child she lives in Palo Alto with an aunt or a stepmother, Rod isn't sure which. The woman's name is Constance, different last name, can't remember what it is. Amanda dropped out of UCLA film school during her freshman year. Work? None that Rod knows of but she always seemed to have money.

"When was the last time you saw her?" Hayes asks.

"Last night," Rod replies. He recounts the argument.

"So she left around seven thirty and you never saw her again."

"That's right."

"And before that?"

"Maybe three weeks ago. That's when I got the restraining order," Rod says. "I thought that had solved the problem. Obviously I was wrong."

I check my watch. It reads five after nine. I tap Rod on the arm and show him the time. He looks over at Hayes.

"As I told you, I'm due in makeup at nine-thirty, Sergeant," Rod says.

"Well, I'm not through with you yet," Hayes says.

"I think you are," I interrupt authoritatively. "My client has been more than cooperative, Sergeant, and now he has to get to work. Unless of course you are planning to arrest him at this moment." I have picked up a lot of law in my writing career and I know that so far Hayes has little to hold him. Hayes knows it, too.

"If I need you, where can I find you?"

"The old Gaffney house by the bay. We'll be there all day."

"I know the place," Hayes says. "Okay, you can go, Mr. Taylor, but your car stays."

"Understood. I'll call the production office for a ride."

"I'll drive you," I pipe up.

"Not necessary, Joe," he says.

"It'll give us a chance to talk."

"Then, fine."

We get up from the table. Hayes fixes me with a hard stare.

"Mr. Bernardi, I'm holding you personally responsible for your client's availability. If he disappears, I'll come looking for you."

"I'd expect nothing less, Sergeant," I reply.

I check at the desk and extend our room for another night, then call Bunny and tell her what's going on, omitting the gory details of the body in the trunk. A few minutes later, Rod and I are on the road heading toward the water and the Gaffney house, a deserted home at the edge of the bay which will serve as Mitch Brenner's home which he shares with his mother and sister.

Sitting in the passenger seat, Rod stares straight ahead, grim faced.

"My God," he says quietly. "She was just a kid. She didn't deserve that."

"But you didn't kill her."

"No, I didn't," Rod says, turning toward me. "But someone did and whoever it is is going to a lot of trouble to make it look that way."

# CHAPTER THREE

Turn left. Right at the stop sign. At the end of the road turn right. Rod's directions are sure and precise. I can see the bay ahead. We round a bend and the house looms up in front of us.

"Park by the motor homes behind the phony shed," Rod says. On my look, he adds, "Built especially for the production, don't ask me why."

I pull up near a Cadillac stretch limo, Hitchcock's transportation, no doubt. The place is alive with activity from the skilled technicians to the laborers who were hired locally to do grunt work. Down at water's edge a half dozen men are constructing a dock that reaches slightly into the bay. The extensive lawn looks so green I'd swear it was painted. It isn't. It's freshly laid sod. Another batch of workers, men and women, are planting full grown flowers and bushes everywhere.

"I need to find Jim Brown and report in," Rod says. Brown is the assistant director and we've already agreed to remain silent about this morning's calamity unless and until it's brought up by others. Sadly, I don't think it will take that long for the word to get out. Rod moves toward the encampment of motorhomes and equipment trailers while I wander toward the house. Just then a vivacious blonde in a mink coat emerges from the front door and starts in my direction. Tippi Hedren. I recognize her right away. It's mutual. She throws me a million dollar smile.

"Hi, gorgeous," I say.

"Hiya, Joe." she says, giving me a big hug.

"How's it going? Having fun or overwhelmed?"

"A little of each," she says. "I used to think modeling was tough. Can't wait till tomorrow. My afternoon off. I get one a week, you know. Master's orders." She shoots a glance toward a nearby shade tree where Hitchcock is deep in conversation with a man I do not know. Hitch glances in our direction. Tippi quickly looks away.

"How's Bertha?"

"Great."

"Somebody said you'd retired."

"Semi. Now I mostly write novels. And, come to think of it, also a screenplay.

"Did you have anything to do with this script?"

"No, but I know the man who did."

"Then you haven't seen the rushes."

"No. Sorry."

"I'd love to know how I'm doing. Most days Hitch says I'm doing just fine but other days, well, I just don't know."

"Just jitters," I say.

"You're probably right."

"How are you getting along with the crew?"

"Wonderful. They're a great bunch."

"And Rod?"

"He's been wonderful to me."

"No, I meant has he had any run-ins with anybody?"

"None I know of," Tippi says. "But wouldn't he have told you if he had?"

"Not a chance," I say. "It's a guy thing."

She laughs. "Yes, I forgot about those guy things. Well, nice talking to you, Joe, but I'm due for a wardrobe fitting. See you later."

"Great." I say as she scurries away. I look back at Hitch. He's staring at me, unsmiling, and when our eyes meet, he does not look away. I do.

An hour passes. I chat with a few of the crew members. I spent a few minutes pumping Norman Deming, the production manager, the man who had been earlier conversing with Hitchcock. Predictably, Deming is overworked, understaffed with a hundred niggling details to worry about. The latest seems to be the local labor force which is agonizingly unreliable. They hire on, work a couple of days, then disappear never to be seen again. One doesn't even pick up his paycheck. Aside from the shirkers, he says, things are moving along well enough. No, there's been no real trouble on the set. Taylor? He gets along with everyone. What's the problem? I don't tell him.

Gracie Something-or-other, crack newspaper photographer, is again on the scene, shooting everything in sight. I walk over to her and when she sees me coming, she rips off a shot of my mug.

"Joe Bernardi," I say to her, "in case you want to add my name to a caption. Novelist, screenwriter, friend of Rod Taylor, Tippi Hedren and Alfred Hitchcock."

"Thanks," she says.

"And you are?"

"Gracie James. Nice to meet you."

"Who's the spread for?" I ask.

"The Santa Rosa Press-Democrat but it's on spec. They get first look but it's non-exclusive. I also sell to a few of the local weeklies."

"Enterprising."

"I try. Got anything for me?"

"Like what?"

"Gossip. Dirt."

"You mean, human interest," I tell her.

"Yeah, that too. You think you could get me ten or fifteen minutes with Taylor? I saw you drive up with him."

"I don't know," I temporize.

"My guy walked out on me six weeks ago and I gotta make a living."

"Okay. I'll see what I can do."

She beams. "Thanks, Joe. You're a peach. Catch you later." She hurries off toward a nearby shade tree where a grey haired woman is sitting, skimming a book. I recognize Jessica Tandy immediately. I look around. No sign of her meddling husband, Hitchcock's muse.

It's a shade past noon. Burks is shooting establishing shots of the Gaffney house, some of which will be used to create process plates for shooting back at the Universal lot. A dark blue Oldsmobile appears and heads for the parking area next to the shed. The security officer is on top of it even before the car comes to a full stop. A woman, maybe five-six and 200 pounds if she's an ounce steps out of the car. A spirited argument ensues. Voices are raised. I'm at the craft services table munching on a tuna salad sandwich. Norman Deming is cracking a hard-boiled egg. When he sees what's happening, he mutters "Shit" and abandons his egg, heading toward the confrontation. I tag along.

"I tried to stop her, sir," the security guard says. "I've told her it's a closed set."

"Are you in charge?" the woman asks brusquely.

"I am," Deming replies, "and you are trespassing."

"Hardly. I am Henrietta Boyle, Assistant District Attorney for Sonoma County. And you are?"

"Norman Deming, unit production manager."

"Excellent. Please direct me to Mr. Rodney Taylor."

"He's busy."

"We'll see about that."

Hoping to still roiling waters, I jump in.

"Maybe I can help. I'm Joe Bernardi."

She turns, arches an eyebrow and fixes me with an evil eye.

"Oh, yes, the attorney," she says.

"Let me talk to the lady, Norman," I say. "I think I can help her and you're busy."

"Sure, Joe, but no visitors, no gawkers. I don't care if she's Pat Brown's mistress." He looks her up and down, then turns and walks off. Good. I'm pretty sure I know why she's here. I'm trying to delay the inevitable.

"I checked with your office in Los Angeles, Mr. Bernardi," Boyle says. "They were astounded that you had passed the bar so quickly and so easily."

"A white lie designed to slow down that county sheriff who seemed much too anxious to drag out his handcuffs."

She nods slowly. "Milt Hayes is a staunch advocate of law and order. Occasionally he becomes over zealous. Where's Taylor?"

"He's busy. Talk to me."

"And why should I do that?"

"Because I have a vested interest in Mr. Taylor's freedom and I can help you or hinder you. Up to you."

"I need to take Mr. Taylor's statement."

"I can arrange it as soon as he's free. Where are you in your investigation?"

Boyle hesitates, regarding me through slitted, suspicious eyes.

"Identification in her purse confirms that her name is Amanda Broome, twenty years old, home address in Palo Alto. Her body has been transported to the morgue in Santa Rosa for autopsy and her aunt has been notified. She is on her way to formally identify the decedent."

"Constance."

"That's right. Constance Perry. You know her?"

"Rod mentioned her name in passing. I've never met her."

We start to walk toward the area where the motorhomes and equipment trucks are gathered.

"What else might Mr. Taylor have mentioned in passing?" she demands to know.

"Not much outside of the restraining order."

"Yes, we checked on that. It was granted three weeks ago. Anything else?"

"No."

"Then I'd like to speak with Mr. Taylor. Now."

"To arrest him?"

"Not yet. Sergeant Hayes is interviewing hotel guests and the forensic people are still going over the car."

I look past her and spot Rod emerging from his motorhome. He sees me and waves. I wave back. No time like the present. I know he has nothing to hide and if we start to stonewall this woman, we are just going to heighten her suspicions. I wave him toward us.

A few minutes later Rod and Henrietta Boyle are in his motorhome. I was told my presence was not required so now I am down at water's edge, looking across the bay toward the town.

To say that I'm troubled is an understatement. The situation is ugly. Very ugly. When the press learns what's happened, they'll slobber all over this story like a Thanksgiving dinner. Beautiful young girl, throat slashed, movie star implicated by secret witness. It has all the elements but only Hitchcock could love this kind of publicity. The truth is, the story could ruin Rod's career. Even when proved innocent, he would always be the actor with the girl's bloody body in the trunk of his car. I think I know Rod well enough to know he didn't do it and that's what's so chilling. Someone is going to a great deal of trouble to frame him for murder and I have no idea who, or more to the point, why. One thing is for certain. Rod's involvement has to be kept secret from the public for as long as possible.

Just then I look back and see Rod and Boyle emerging from his motorhome. He heads toward the house, she walks toward her car. I jog across the lawn to the parking area and arrive just as she's reaching for her car door handle.

"How did your meeting go?" I ask.

"Unproductive."

"Ms. Boyle, I am relying on you to keep this investigation as fair and as low key and as discreet as possible. Rod Taylor is not your run of the mill street bum."

"I understand that," she says.

"Then understand this. Any action on your part, short of an arrest, which results in Mr. Taylor being negatively portrayed in the press will result in very harsh and expensive litigation brought against you, your office and the county."

"That sounds like a threat."

"It is. Any mention of Mr. Taylor's name can only be for the purposes of publicity and/or self-aggrandizment and if you think Universal Studios is going to quietly let this motion picture be destroyed by a publicity seeking officer of the court, you are sadly mistaken."

"I don't work that way, Mr. Bernardi." she says.

"See that you don't," I say and turn on my heel and head for my car.

Bunny is unhappy. I knew she would be.

"What do you mean, you want us to go back to L.A.? We're on vacation. It just started."

"I know but there are things I have to do and you and Yvette are just going to be in the way."

We're keeping our voices down because Yvette is in the bathroom, door closed, soaking in the tub.

"I won't be in the way," comes a squeaky voice from behind the door.

"Now you've done it," Bunny whispers.

"Sorry," I whisper back, "but Rod's in trouble and if I don't help him the local gendarmes are going to railroad him right into San Quentin."

Her eyes widen.

"The parking lot. This morning this cop knocks on my door, wants to know if I saw anything going on in the parking lot last night. Something about a dead body stuffed in a trunk. I told him I went to sleep early and woke up late. That seemed to satisfy him and he left. Joe, what's going on?"

I tell her. She can't believe it.

"Impossible," she says.

"I know but as some writer once said, the law is an ass and I have to make sure Rod doesn't become front page news and who better than me to see to It. After all, it was my livelihood for sixteen years."

"It could get dangerous," Bunny says.

"I doubt it but I still have my gun and I still have my permit."

She snorts. "Gun. It's an overgrown cap pistol with delusions of fire power."

Bunny, like my close friend Lt. Aaron Kleinschmidt of Los Angeles Homicide, loves to demean my .25 caliber automatic Beretta. I ignore them both.

"I'm going to drive over to Santa Rosa and see what I can learn about the autopsy and the forensics. It's a short drive. I should be back by dinner. Unless there's a miraculous break in this case, tomorrow morning I'm going to put you and Yvette on a plane back to L.A."

"Joe—"

"No argument, Bunny. Aside from the fact that I need Rod for my movie, a minor consideration, he's a terrific guy who doesn't deserve what's happening. Or maybe you think I should just walk away."

She hesitates, then says, "No, of course I don't."

"Good girl," I say, taking her in my arms and kissing her warmly.

Just then Yvette emerges from the bathroom, takes one look, says "Yuck" and goes back inside.

# CHAPTER FOUR

I check with the front desk for directions and then head for Santa Rosa. It's about twenty miles as the crow flies but I'm no crow and the first few miles to Sebastopol are slow going over rutted back roads designed to rattle loose the bolts on the sturdiest of vehicles. After that it's straight into Santa Rosa on Route 12, a marked improvement. I stop at the first service station on the outskirts of the city and get directions to the city and county offices which are located on Administration Drive just off Highway 101.

Santa Rosa is quaint and sleepy. Twenty years ago it was even more so when Hitchcock filmed 'Shadow of a Doubt' here with Joe Cotten and Teresa Wright. Some towns age well. Santa Rosa is one of them. It takes me only fifteen minutes to locate the building housing the District Attorney's office where I set off in search of Henrietta Boyle.

I'm crossing the lobby heading for the elevator to the second floor when a familiar figure cuts in front of me.

"Surprise, surprise," Sergeant Hayes says with an insincere smile," if it isn't my favorite lawyer."

"Good afternoon, Sergeant," I say.

"Good for you, counselor. Not so good for the young lady in the trunk. By the way, where did you get your law degree? Woolworth's?

The May Company? You never did say."

"I'm sorry about that little deception. I know you were just doing your job but your attitude was more accusatory than inquisitive. I felt obliged to step in."

"I could have you arrested for hindering a police investigation," Hayes says.

I hold my hands out in front of me.

"Do your duty," I say.

He shakes his head in disgust.

"You really are something of a wise apple, Bernardi. What are you doing here?"

"Hoping to get some information," I say, withdrawing my hands.

He jerks his head sideways.

"The information desk is to your left."

"I'm wondering what your forensic people might have found."

"Keep wondering. This is a murder investigation and none of your business."

"I guess Mr. Taylor had better get himself a lawyer then."

"Be dumb if he didn't," Hayes says with a crooked smile. "Have a nice day, Mr. Bernardi," he adds as he brushes past me and heads for the main entrance.

The gatekeeper on the second floor is no help. I ask to see Ms. Boyle. No, I don't have an appointment. Sorry, she's tied up in a meeting. I'll wait. It may be a while. I'll wait anyway, say I, and pull up a sofa. I start to leaf through a copy of a travel magazine extolling the virtues of Guam. Six minutes later Boyle appears, walking toward the elevator accompanied by an elegantly dressed woman with light brown hair just starting to grey. Boyle and I exchange looks as the woman gets on the elevator. I suspect who she is. I need confirmation. I get up and smoothly walk in Boyle's direction. I start to speak. She beats me to it.

"I have no time for you, Mr. Bernardi," she says, brushing past me.

"Not even a kind word?"

She turns and looks back at me.

"Go back to Bodega. You're wasting my time and yours. Even if I had learned something new, which I haven't, I am certainly not going to share it with you. Give my regards to Mr. Taylor. Tell him I'll be in touch."

With that she continues down the hall. Obviously the woman is going to share nothing. A different tack is needed. I open the door marked 'Stairs' and dash down, two steps at a time. When I emerge from the building, I spot Boyle's visitor walking toward the parking lot. I hurry to catch up.

"Mrs. Perry?" I say loudly. She turns and I get a closer look. I put Constance Perry close to 50. Her features are chiseled but not unattractive and she wears a minimum of makeup. Even a fashion dolt like me can see she is expensively garbed in white silk and there is nothing cheap about her emerald necklace and earrings. She regards me curiously.

"My name is Joe Bernardi. I'm a friend of Rod Taylor's."

"Are you." A statement. Her expression is cold, her attitude imperious.

"Please accept my sympathies on the death of your niece. I was hoping you could spare me a few minutes to talk."

"About what?"

"I want to assure you that Mr. Taylor had nothing to do with Amanda's death."

"That remains to be seen, Mr..."

"Bernardi."

"In any case, I'm in a hurry. I have to check into my hotel."

"Oh? Where are you staying?"

"That, sir, is none of your business."

She turns and walks away. I hurry to catch up.

"Please," I say. "Just a couple of minutes. You may know something that—"

"Young man, I know absolutely nothing and I think I have made it clear I have nothing to say to you. I have suffered an excruciating loss, a dear child that I have raised since the age of six, a sweet thing whom I held dear even during the darkest of times. I have no idea how I am going to cope but cope I will. Now please demonstrate some compassion and leave me be."

With that she strides off toward a Forest Green Lincoln town car where a liveried chauffeur is standing by. A tall sturdy looking man with a cold visage and an ugly scar running down his neck just below his left ear lobe. I would suspect that he doubles as a bodyguard. Any other duties he might have regarding Constance Perry's well-being I would rather not contemplate. He opens the rear door even as he stares at me with a malevolent expression. She gets in. A moment later the car is headed out of the parking lot. Uneasily I watch her go. Her words were passionate but she was not. I saw not a glimmer of a tear, not a glimpse of true sorrow. Who is this woman and what is she made of? All sorts of conflicting thoughts are swirling around in my brain. Getting to the truth about Amanda Broome's death may be a lot more difficult than I bargained for.

I head back to Bodega and since it is still light, I drive straight to the set to tell Rod what I didn't learn on my wasted trip to Santa Rosa. Jim Brown, the A.D. tells me Rod was released a half hour ago. I spot Bob Burks and his crew shooting nothing but scenery and surmise this footage will be used for process plates. Process plates are used for projection on a screen, then putting a live scene in front of it giving the impression that the scene was shot entirely on location when actually it wasn't. I turn to go when I spot Hitchcock standing on the front porch of the house, beckoning me to join him. I do so and he suggests we go inside.

As we step into the living room, he looks around making certain we are alone, then points to the sofa where I sit. He plops down on an easy chair close by and leans forward, speaking quietly.

"I have been reliably informed," he says, "that Mr. Taylor may be in some trouble with the local authorities. True or not, Joe?"

"True," I say, "but for the moment, nothing for you to worry about."

He arches an eyebrow.

"I am concerned about that phrase, 'for the moment'. Please elucidate."

I tell him what I know. He is surprised and concerned. He had heard only a hint of trouble, certainly nothing of this magnitude and no, to the best of his knowledge, the cast and crew know nothing of Rod's predicament.

"Then let's try to keep it that way, Hitch," I say. "I have threatened the authorities with the seven plagues of Egypt if even a whisper of this reaches the press but sooner or later it'll get out unless the actual perpetrator can be unmasked beforehand."

"Silence shall be my watchword," Hitchcock says. "Is there anything I can or should do?"

"No, you have enough to deal with. I'm going to dig deep and see if I can learn anything helpful."

"Quebec City redux," he says with a twinkle.

"Seems so."

When we were shooting 'I Confess' in Canada, I got embroiled in a murder which threatened to shut down the picture. I got to the bottom of it and ever since Hitch has had great admiration for my cognitive powers.

I get up to go but he stops me.

"Sit down, Joe. Another topic." I sit. "You may have heard that my relationship with Miss Hedren is untypical. It is but I want to assure you that it is strictly professional. I have been forced to employ unusual tactics to get the most out of her. When dealing with Miss Kelly or Miss Novak or Miss Bergman, I was blessed with experienced, consummate performers. Miss Hedren is lovely and eager but undisciplined. I try not to be harsh but I am firm and I am demanding and this approach shows in her work which improves each day."

"I would never question your methods or your motives, Hitch."

"Thank you, Joe. I was sure you wouldn't. Now hurry off to that wife of yours and try to keep me apprised of this business with Mr. Taylor whenever you can."

I find Bunny in the room fixing her hair. Yvette is camped out in front of the television set watching The Three Stooges batter each other around.

"We're having dinner again with Rod tonight," Bunny smiles.

"Well, that'll be a lot of laughs," I reply glumly.

"What? No luck?"

"None," I say. "Tomorrow or the next day, this is going to blow up and Rod's face is going to be plastered all over the front page of every newspaper in the country."

"That bad?"

"I threatened Ms. Boyle with Lew Wasserman but she didn't seem to care about Universal's clout. Rod needs a tough son of a bitch to represent him and he needs him now."

"Call Ray."

"My thoughts exactly."

I sit on the edge of the bed and dial Ray Giordano at his Westwood home. Ray is L.A.'s preeminent defense attorney. The mere mention of his name drives wooden stakes into the hearts of prosecutors everywhere in Southern California. Happily he and I have been friends for almost twenty years. To my surprise I find him home and quickly explain my problem. I need him and I need him now.

"Can't help you, Joe. I'm hip deep in a trial defending some scuzzy financial advisor."

"Why is it all your clients are scuzzy, Ray?"

"Because they pay well, my idealistic friend, and besides, a few of them are even innocent."

"Bullshit."

"Perhaps misunderstood, then."

"In your dreams."

"Let's not quibble. Now if I understand you correctly, you need a bona fide take-no-prisoners shark to represent Mr. Taylor."

"And I need him tomorrow."

"Yes, yes, I got all that," Ray says. "And this is where? Santa Rosa? Sonoma County?"

"Right."

There's a few moments of silence and then Ray says, "I know someone. Ezra Crabtree. Born with a wooden stick up his ass and to the best of my knowledge he's never lost a case to a Sonoma County D.A."

"I love him already."

"What's your number there?" I tell him. "Okay, stick by the phone. In a few minutes either I'll call you back or you'll hear from Ezra."

"Ten-four," I say, hanging up and beginning my vigil with a cold Nehi from the minibar. At 5:14 the phone rings and I quickly pick up.

"Mr. Bernardi, Ezra Crabtree here. Raymond Giordano asked me to call you." His voice is crackly and as dry as stale bread. I picture an old man ready for retirement.

"Yes. Thanks for getting back to me so quickly." I say.

"So I take it you're in deep trouble with the county's D.A. office."

"Not me. The actor Rod Taylor. He's here in Bodega Bay shooting a movie with Alfred Hitchcock."

"Never heard of this Taylor fella. Hitchcock? He the chubby guy with the television program?"

"That's right."

"Don't watch much TV. Movies either. Tell me again what the problem is." I go through it slowly and concisely. When I mention Sergeant Hayes, Crabtree grunts. Tough but fair. When I mention Henrietta Boyle, he jumps in loudly. "That bitch? By God, Mr. Bernardi, you've made my day. Sticking it to that publicity-seeking cow is a hobby of mine. You're staying at the Bodega Bay Arms?"

"Yes."

"I'll meet you there for dinner at seven. Have Mr. Taylor with you." Click. He hangs up. I look over at Bunny.

"I think Rod has himself a lawyer," I tell her.

Ezra Crabtree is nothing like I'd imagined. Mid to late 30's, thinning blonde hair atop a skinny hawk-like face, his deep set brown eyes seem to miss nothing. While we eat, he grills Rod mercilessly, occasionally making a note in a pad at his elbow. Rod repeats what he told me and not much more and by the time dessert rolls around, Crabtree puts away his notepad, apparently satisfied.

"First thing in the morning, I'll call on Henrietta, hopefully before breakfast so I can spoil her appetite," Crabtree says and then allows himself to smile. "I can shut her up, Mr. Taylor, but not forever and if you are arrested, all bets are off. But unless there's something you're not telling me—"

"There isn't."

"Then I doubt she has enough for an arrest and she knows if she jumps the gun without enough evidence, I will crucify her for false arrest. Now, who's going to buy me a brandy?"

The next morning I drive Bunny and Yvette to the Santa Rosa airport to catch a Hughes Airwest flight to San Francisco where they will connect to a flight to LAX. Bunny doesn't want to go but she understands there are things I need to do that she can't be any part of. I feel like Bogey blowing off Bergman at the Casablanca airport. Yvette, too, is disappointed until Bunny promises that she and Bridget, our housekeeper, will take her to Disneyland tomorrow. At that point, I become an impediment, best ignored.

I wave goodbye as the plane lifts off, then head for the parking lot and the thirty mile drive south to Palo Alto. I'm not sure what I expect to find there but Constance Perry's frosty and almost secretive attitude hint that maybe the answer to Amanda Broome's death lies in her home town. It's a Thursday. I figure I have two days, maybe three, before a janitor at the D.A.'s office hears something he shouldn't, passes it along to his wife who blabs it to her sewing circle. At that point, game over. I pull out of the airport parking lot, head south on Route 101, ignoring the speed limit whenever I can. Time is not on my side.

# CHAPTER FIVE

I roll into Palo Alto a few minutes before noon and the first thing I do is look for a book store. It doesn't take long and I get lucky. They have two copies of "A Family of Strangers" and I buy one of them. The gawky clerk starts to ring it up, then notices my photo on the back cover. He gives me a funny look.

"I was thinner then," I say with a smile. He half-smiles back, rings up my $11.95 and hands me change from a twenty. He neglects to ask for my autograph. I ask where I can find the local library. He has no clue but I'll bet he knows where the local comic book emporium is located.

I head for my car, ask directions of a passing mother wheeling her baby carriage and she gives me precise directions to the library, not more than five blocks away. I take a left, then a right and there it is, a small but attractive building on a green plot of land. I exit the Bentley and go inside, my book tucked under my arm. I ask for the head librarian and the clerk at the checkout desk points out a matronly lady sitting at a desk in a far corner.

She looks up with a smile as I approach. She's white haired with a round pleasant face behind wire-rimmed glasses. The name on her desk plaque reads Mae Unger and a small brown bag is propped up beside it.

"Is that Ms. or Mrs. Unger?" I ask.

"Who cares?" she says. "Call me Mae."

"Call me Joe," I reply, presenting her with the book which I have already autographed. "A small contribution to your stacks."

She takes it, notes the inscription and checks out my picture on the back of the dust jacket. "Oh,my, this is an honor. Thank you, Mr. Bernardi."

"Joe. Remember."

"Yes, Of course. I loved this book, Joe. Also your new one. Quite different but just as good a read."

"Thank you, Mae. Are you a native?"

"Born in Sacramento, moved here when I was six, just in time for first grade."

"Then you're just the person I want to talk to. I'm researching my new book using Santa Rosa as the background and if anyone can help me, I'm sure it's you."

"I'd be delighted to help any way I can."

I point to the brown bag.

"Your lunch?"

"Egg salad and a yogurt."

"Dump it. I'm taking you to lunch."

"Oh, no, that isn't necessary."

"My pleasure, Mae, and no argument. Name it."

Mother Banyon's Cafe isn't fancy but it's cozy and the owner, Lily Banyon, and Mae are like blood sisters. We get a lovely table for two looking out over a garden and a pretty young third generation Banyon named Jamie waits on our table. The atmosphere is hushed and we can talk without raising our voices. I order a cold Coors, Mae opts for an Old Fashioned and after Jamie trots off with our lunch order, we start to chat about the town, the weather, and other topics of no consequence.

"So, Mae, tell me about Amanda Broome," I say, finally getting to the point of our luncheon.

"Oh, that one," she says raising her eyes to heaven. "Wild as a she-wolf in heat." She hesitates. "Why ask about her? Isn't this a novel you're working on, Joe?"

"Fiction mixed with fact to give it some authenticity. I have a friend who shares your view of her. I'll probably make passing mention of her."

Mae snorts. "You could write a whole book about her, Joe, and not cover everything. A shame the way she turned out but I suppose it was inevitable. If only her father hadn't died when she was so young, she might have had a decent upbringing."

"Her father? Sorry, don't know a thing about him," I say.

"Andrew. Lovely man. Charming and smart as a whip. Famous in some circles as well. He invented some kind of device the Navy used during the war and after the Japanese surrendered, he started his own company and made a fortune."

"Funny I never heard of him," I say.

Mae smiles. "The war made millionaires of a lot of men, Joe. Many were war profiteers, a few like Andrew were real patriots. You would have called him a very blessed man but in 1947 his wife died of pneumonia and two years later, he was killed when he surprised a burglar trying to ransack his house. Amanda was seven years old when that woman moved into the house and took over."

"Constance Perry," I say.

"You've met her."

"Sadly, yes," I reply.

"She was Andrew's sister and his only living relative outside of Amanda."

"And Constance raised Amanda."

"I wouldn't say that. She let Amanda run wild, no discipline, no restraints. Whatever Amanda wanted she got. Money was not a problem. Andrew left behind a substantial estate."

"To who? Constance or Amanda?"

"No one really knows for sure. Constance was the executrix of the will and I suppose Amanda's legal guardian. I believe there's some sort of trust fund for the girl but as I said, Joe, no one really knows."

"Constance. Does she work?"

"Oh, no."

"She doesn't seem to be hurting for money."

"I suppose Andrew provided for her. And I understand executors receive some sort of compensation."

"If so, it must be substantial. There must have been a lawyer as well."

"I suppose there was. I don't remember. It was fourteen years ago. Poirot would say my little grey cells are losing their way."

I smile at her. "I doubt that, Mae. So, about Constance. Where does the last name Perry fit in? Is she married?"

"Was," Mae says. "Roy Perry teaches Business Administration locally. Smart fella. Got a PhD from Penn State and he's written three books, you know."

"No, I didn't know."

"We have copies of all of them. Oh, yes, everybody hereabouts knows Roy. Been living here for years. He's an older man. Older than her, anyway. As I recall he was 40 and a widower with a three year old son when they got married just before the war. It didn't last long. Roy's a gentle thoughtful man, Mr. Bernardi. Constance was, and is—well, you met her. By the time the Japanese surrendered, they were divorced. I think it was a great relief for them both."

Jamie appears with our orders. I dig into a platter of fried clams. Mae daintily pokes at her Cobb salad and orders another old fashioned.

"About Amanda," I say, "as wild as she was, did she have a lot of friends or did she make a lot of enemies?"

"Oh, I wouldn't know anything about that. I know she was arrested three or four times, mostly for public intoxication. I know they eventually barred her from The Pig Sty."

"Pig Sty?"

"A hangout for youngsters and wannabe youngsters. All the kids go there, even those underage. They're lax about checking ID."

"Gotcha."

"The second time, when she was tossed out for good, the police picked her up and held her all night in the jail. The next day, she scooted."

"Scooted?"

"Left town. Two years ago, I think. Quit her second year of UCLA with some wild idea of becoming a movie star. I'm not sure anyone's heard from her since. Kids, Joe. Makes me glad I never married. I hear it all the time. They drive you crazy or break your heart and often both at the same time."

I ask a couple more questions about Amanda and I see in Mae's eyes a growing suspicion that I have ulterior motives in taking her to lunch. Since Amanda's death is not yet common knowledge I want to keep it that way for as long as possible and besides, I'm pretty sure Mae doesn't have anything more to contribute. Throughout lunch we chat casualty about the city which boasts a high median income, a highly educated populace and is home to Stanford University. President Herbert Hoover was a Palo Alto native as was Perry Mason creator Erle Stanley Gardner. All food for a book I have no intention of writing.

I have her back at the library by one-thirty and as she waves from the doorway and goes inside, I contemplate my next move. Constance Perry is at the top of my list but before I confront her, I want to be armed with something besides my Italian good looks. All this talk of estates and executors and possible trust funds has aroused my instinctively suspicious nature. There's a ton of money involved in all this and I find that where money is involved, skullduggery often abounds. I am pretty sure there was a lawyer involved at the time of Andrew Broome's death and I am also pretty sure I need to speak to him.

I remember a phone booth on the corner next to the restaurant and I drive back there. The yellow pages are hanging on a chain and I thumb through to 'Newspapers' where I find an address for the Palo Alto Weekly. The city map up front tells me how to find Cambridge Avenue and six minutes later, I'm walking in the front door. The young guy behind the counter with the Tab Hunter buzz cut smiles when I ask to speak to the editor.

"At your service, sir," he says. I was expecting Lionel Barrymore, not his grandson.

"I need a little help. I'm a writer and I'm researching a murder that took place here in Palo Alto about thirteen years ago."

He shakes his head apologetically.

"I'm afraid that's a little before my time," he says.

"Broome murder. August 3, 1949. Am I right, sonny?"

The voice, more like a cackle, comes from across the room. An old timer with a green eyeshade is sitting at a desk. Wizened and white-haired he looks more like Percy Kilbride than Barrymore but he'll do.

"That's right," I say.

"Got copies in the basement. Special tenth anniversary edition we put out in '59. Before your time, Biff. Reprinted the original issue word for word,. Come on, I'll show you."

He gets up and I follow him to a staircase. We go down into the basement which is dry and dim but not dank and the old fellow knows right where to go. He unfolds the flaps of a cardboard carton and extracts a four-page copy of the newspaper. It's yellowing slightly but highly readable. The headline is lurid. BROOME SLAIN IN HOUSE BREAK-IN. A photo of a rugged middle-aged man with an easy smile dominates the middle of the page.

"May I take this with me?" I ask.

"Sure."

"How much do I owe you?"

"Nothin', sonny. Pleasure to be of service."

"Well, thank you, Mr.—?"

"Perkins. Del Perkins. That's my byline right there." He proudly points it out. "Helluva story. I was only here a year when it happened. A lot different than writing up some thirteen year old brat's bar mitzvah."

We start back up the stairs.

"Maybe you could tell me who Andrew Broome's lawyer was at the time."

"It'll be in there. As I recall it was Malachi Crown but don't hold me to it."

"Is he still around?"

"I believe he is but he gave up lawyerin' a while back. Lives on the north part of town, him and his wife, Charlene.

We reach the ground floor and I shake the old timer's hand.

"Thanks for the courtesy, Mr. Perkins. I'm looking forward to reading this."

"Take care now," he says.

As I head for the front door, I lean in toward Biff, the youthful editor, and whisper, "He's a keeper, that one. Don't let him get away."

"Thanks," Biff says, giving me a perplexed look.

Outside, I slip behind the wheel of the Bentley and start to read. Twenty minutes later I've absorbed the essentials. Somewhere around nine o'clock Broome returned home from an emergency business meeting with several corporate officers. Apparently he surprised a burglar trying to break into a wall safe in his study. The painting that had hidden the safe had been taken down, a wooden mallet and a steel chisel were found on the floor and gouge marks were found on the safe's hinges. At nine-thirty or so, Constance Perry, Broome's sister, arrived home, driven there by close friend Isobel Graham. The lights were all on. The front door was wide open. Sensing something wrong, the two women hurried inside to find Broome dead on the study floor, shot twice. Police were called and arrived twelve minutes later. A house search was made for the murder weapon but it was not found.

Toward the end of the article I find Malachi Crown's name. My next move is obvious. It's vital that I talk to this lawyer. I go in search of another phone booth.

Crown must have been a hell of a lawyer because his home is a sprawling ranch house on an immaculately kept grassy acre at the north end of town. I park on the street and walk up a flagstone path to the front door. I push the doorbell and a few moments later the door is opened by an attractive older woman whom I immediately surmise to be his wife. She displays a curious but guarded smile. I get the feeling that the Crowns don't get much company, especially from strangers.

"Mrs. Crown?"

"Yes."

"My name is Joseph Bernardi. I apologize for showing up without warning but I drove down here on a matter of some importance from Santa Rosa. I need to speak to your husband."

"I'm sorry, Mr. Bernardi, but Malachi is not receiving visitors."

I grimace."Oh, my. As I said, this is a matter of the gravest importance and I won't take up much of his time."

"I regret having to be rude, sir, but it is quite impossible."

"It involves a murder, ma'am."

"Are you with the police?"

"No, I'm not and for the moment I'd prefer they not get involved."

She forces a smile. "Whether they do or they don't won't make much difference. All right, Mr. Bernardi. Come in."

I thank her and step inside. She leads me into the living room where a bank of sliding glass doors look out onto a brick patio and a view of the hills in the distance. An old man sits slumped in a wheelchair, staring straight ahead and if he has any idea of his surroundings, he doesn't show it.

"You can speak to him if you wish but most days he doesn't even know his own name."

I stare sadly at this wreck of a man swathed in a blanket and my heart goes out to him and to his wife.

"I'm so sorry," I say. "How long—?

"Almost a year now. We sit out on the porch in the evening and I tell him about my day. Some nights I think he hears me and understands. Others—?" She merely shrugs. "His heart is strong and his lungs are good but nonetheless, he's dying, Mr. Bernardi, hour by hour, day by day, but it won't be quick. It is a terrible way to exist for both of us but I can't imagine living without him."

"I understand."

"Then you must be happily married," she observes warmly.

"Decidedly so," I smile. "Is there someone else I can talk to, Mrs. Crown? Someone who worked for him back then?"

Now it's her turn to smile.

"Would his personal secretary of twenty-seven years do?"

"Perfect," I say. "Where can I find her?"

"You're looking at her," Charlene Crown says.

# CHAPTER SIX

"So what you're telling us is, the old lady gets the money," Rod says, twirling his spaghetti with his fork.

"Every last dime, according to Charlene Crown and she ought to know," I say as I cut into my sirloin and find it perfectly medium rare.

It's a few minutes to eight. We are gathered in the restaurant at the Bodega Bay Arms. Bunny is nibbling at a Nicoise salad and Ezra Crabtree, who spent the late afternoon in consultation with Rod, has opted for liver and onions. Yvette is in the room with yet another hamburger, watching 'The Adventures of Ozzie and Harriet' and fantasizing about Ricky Nelson.

"Amanda would have turned twenty-one on August 11th," I say, "putting Constance Perry out of her job as executrix and as Amanda's guardian. The terms of the trust put Constance in second position should anything untoward happen to Amanda prior to reaching her majority. To the best of Charlene's recollection, the amount of the trust was originally eighteen million dollars. With interest accrued conservatively over the past thirteen years, that figure could well exceed thirty million."

"Not a bad motive for a homicide," Bunny mutters between bites.

"Unkind, sweetheart," I chide her.

"Unkind but accurate," Ezra says. "I don't suppose Mrs. Perry has an alibi for the time of the murder."

"I didn't ask," I say.

"I'll be seeing Henrietta first thing tomorrow. I'll make sure she asks the question," Ezra chimes in, "though I suspect Mrs. Perry's alibi will be unbreakable."

"Because?" Rod says.

"Because slitting someone's throat is totally out of a character for a woman of Constance Perry's age and social station. Poison, yes. A small caliber pistol, very possibly. But a bloody, gory knifing? Impossible. Besides the woman's no fool. If she is responsible, she'd have had the deed done for her by another while she was establishing that perfect alibi."

"Opening herself up to possible blackmail down the line," I say.

Ezra smiles. "You've been watching too many B-movies, Mr. Bernardi. The lady merely has to hire a second killer to murder the first killer. The second killer, painfully aware of the lengths that the lady will go to to protect herself, will think long and hard about attempting extortion. Do I make sense?"

"Sounds good to me," Rod says.

"This presupposes that the lady is involved," Ezra says, "and we have no proof of that, only a possible motive. Fortunately that is more than enough to direct even a self-absorbed ambitious nincompoop like Henrietta Boyle to look elsewhere instead of automatically draping a noose around Mr. Taylor's neck."

I look past his shoulder to the restaurant entrance and spot a familiar face looking around, obviously searching for someone. Gracie James catches my eye and waves. I wave back, beckoning her to our table. She's still wearing her khakis.

"I hate to interrupt," she says, then looks at Rod. "Can we talk, Mr. Taylor?"

"Sure."

"In private," she says, giving the rest of us a wary look.

"I have no secrets from my friends, Gracie. Pull up a chair."

Hesitantly she does so.

"How about some coffee? Or a drink," I say.

"No. No thanks." She hesitates again, then says, "About an hour ago I was at the newspaper office developing today's work. A phone call came in. Harry Felcher took it. He's one of our reporters. A conceited hotshot. He can't understand why he hasn't yet won a Pulitzer. Harry hung up and grabbed me, said to stay available just in case. He'd just gotten a tip from some guy that there'd been a murder at the Bodega Bay Arms Hotel and the cops were covering it up." She looks at Rod. "He said that Mr. Taylor was involved." She looks around the table at us, awaiting a reaction. "You know about it," she says, staring into our unsmiling faces.

I respond for the group.

"A body was discovered in the trunk of Mr. Taylor's car, Gracie, and the police and the District Attorney's office are investigating. Mr. Taylor hasn't been charged with anything and for obvious reasons, we, all of us, are trying to keep this as quiet as possible, at least for the moment."

"Sure, I get it," Gracie says. "Well, Harry was on the phone trying to reach the Assistant District Attorney but either she was out or she wasn't answering."

"The tipster was a man, you're sure about that?" Ezra says.

"That's what Harry told me."

Ezra stands, tossing his napkin on the table.

"It seems to me that whoever is working this frame is annoyed that the murder has not surfaced and is trying to prod some action. I'm going to drive back to Santa Rosa and camp out on Henrietta's doorstep. She's been warned but Felcher's a bulldog. Our message to her may need reinforcing."

We wish him luck as he heads out. I look over at Bunny. The pressure is building. I check out Rod sitting across from me. He's glumly staring at his unfinished meal. He no longer seems hungry.

Rod's Corvette has been towed to Santa Rosa so early the next morning I drive him to the set. Again the company is shooting at the Gaffney house. He is silent during the drive and I can't blame him. The enormity of his plight is starting to overwhelm him. When we arrive, I drop him at his motorhome and park. I wander toward the house and see that the wharf has been completed and the camera crew is setting up at water's edge for the next scene.

"So what's happening? Where are we?" asks a voice at my side. Norman Deming is sipping coffee and staring at me curiously.

"Where are we what, Norman?" I ask innocently.

"Don't give me that, Bernardi. What do you take me for, a turnip farmer? When Hitch told you he was reliably informed about events, who the hell do you think reliably informed him?"

"And I'd like to know who reliably informed you?"

"I've got a crystal ball," he says. "All us production managers do. It's how we keep our jobs. So?"

"So far the veil of secrecy is holding. I give it a day, two at the outside, then all hell breaks loose."

"And I lose my star. Pretty hard to put together a shooting schedule when your lead actor's in the calaboose."

I nod. "I'm going to drive down to Palo Alto and see what I can do about that."

"What's in Palo Alto?" he asks.

"A killer, maybe. By the way, a hard-nosed reporter named Felcher may try to barge onto the set. Discourage him."

"Set's closed, Mr. Bernardi, and it's going to stay that way. Waldo will see to it. Good luck in Palo Alto." He tosses his paper cup in a nearby trash can and walks off.

I drive into Palo Alto shortly before ten. I find a phone booth next to a service station and call Ezra Crabtree. I get lucky. He's at his desk.

"How'd you make out last night?" I ask him.

"My ass is sore but other than that, we're not yet in trouble. I parked at Henrietta's curbside for over two hours. She finally rolled in just after eleven having been at a private dinner party. Felcher never reached her. I explained the situation. She commiserated. I may not be her favorite person but I'm higher on her Christmas list than Harry Felcher whom she considers a low down, double crossing snake without morals, scruples or any other saving grace. He'll get nothing from her."

"So all we have to worry about is the janitor, the trash collector, a receptionist's hair dresser or some other non-entity who stumbles onto the situation inadvertently."

"Right," Ezra says. "Where are you, by the way?"

"Palo Alto. I'm going to brace Constance Perry. I doubt I'll get a full blown confession but I may get a glimpse of what she's been up to. At the very least I may be able to scare the crap out of her."

"Let me know how that turns out, " Ezra says, his voice exuding sarcasm.

I hang up and walk over to the service station. Sources of information come in a variety of packages. Bartenders top the list followed by the local barber and a librarian. Somewhere in the mix, especially if the needed data is geographical, comes the garage owner. The old timer in the service bay looking up at the undercarriage of a well-traveled Ford Fairlane smiles as I approach.

"Sorry to bother you," I say, "but I seem to be lost. I'm trying to find the old Broome estate."

"North of town. You can't miss it. Take 101 north, get off at Embarcadero which turns in to Sand Hill Road. A quarter of mile on your left, you'll see an old brick Georgian set back on a two acre lot. That'll be it."

I thank him and head back to the car. His directions were precise and twelve minutes later I pull up in front of the imposing edifice that Constance Perry calls home. The property is completely enclosed with wrought iron fencing and giant gates guard the driveway. There is a communication box on the left side pillar. Not convenient for the Bentley. I get out of the car and push the button and then look up at the television camera staring down at me from above. I get no response. I buzz again. Still nothing. I look up the hill and spot Constance's hulking chauffeur who has appeared at the side of the house and is glaring down at me. I press up against the gate and wave at him. He continues to glare, then turns and disappears out of sight. I buzz one more time to no avail. I will not be bracing Constance Perry any time soon, for sure not today.

I get back in the car, make a u-turn and head back toward 101. At a crossroads I spot a directional sign for Stanford University. I hesitate. If I can't speak to the lady herself maybe the discarded ex-husband can impart something I need to know. A few minutes later I'm pulling into a parking space near the Administration Building. The University is everything I thought it would be and then some. Sprawling landscape, beautiful two and three story buildings, well-tended green areas everywhere. Well worth the $2800 a year tuition.

I walk inside and ask the lady at the information desk if Professor Perry is teaching a class today. She stares at me blankly.

"I'm sorry, I don't think we have a Professor Perry," she says.

"Business Administration?"

She shakes her head.

"No, I think not. Just a moment. You may be thinking of another school in the area." She reaches into a drawer and takes out a slim directory. She starts to read through it, then stops. "Roy Perry?"

"That's right."

"He's on the faculty of Foothill College in Los Altos Hills. It's close by. The next town. I can give you directions."

A minute later I'm back in my car and heading southwest to El Monte Rd and Foothill College, a two-year community college. I'm surprised when I turn into the entrance. It's no Stanford but it is large and well kept up with dozens of buildings and lecture halls and on this beautiful May day, the students are out in force, milling about. I pass an athletic field with an huge sign that reads "Home of the Owls". A spirited soccer game is in progress.

Again I check in at Administration. No, Professor Perry has no class at the moment but he can usually be found in his office this time of day. The helpful young lady at the desk (name tag: 'Georgia. How May I Help You') provides me with a map of the campus on which she has planted a red "X" on Perry's office building. Since it's a nice day. I decide to leave the car where it is and hoof it. On the way, I keep wondering why a well-published PhD from Penn State (probably the Wharton School) is teaching at a community college instead of a prestigious institution like Stanford.

I reach the building. Several cars are parked near the entrance including a brand new white Cadillac Coupe deVille with the vanity license plate, "R PERRY". I also notice something else. Affixed to the windshield is a parking permit for the Los Altos Hills Golf and Country Club. Hmm. Maybe I am too quick to regard the good doctor's employment as penury. I walk in, check the directory and climb the stairs to the second floor. I tap on the door to number 202 and a voice from within bids me enter.

He's sitting at his desk, peering at some paperwork through thick-lensed wire rim glasses. He's dressed in shirt sleeves, tie pulled down, a tweed sport jacket with leather elbow patches is hanging on a wooden coat tree in the corner of the room. His hair is a grey-ish brown, tousled and in need of a good combing or a haircut, maybe both. He is the living breathing cliche of the ivory tower college professor. Maybe they all buy their outfits in the same uniform store. As I enter, closing the door behind me, he shoves his glasses up onto his forehead and regards me curiously.

"Yes?"

"I hope I'm not disturbing, Professor."

"No, no, not at all. Come in."

I extend my hand.

"Joe Bernardi."

"Roy Perry. Do sit down, Mr. Bernardi."

"Thank you," I say sitting in the empty chair by his desk. I spot a formidable looking trophy of a golfer in mid-swing sitting on a nearby shelf. I nod toward it. "You golf," I say.

"My son Hank. He gave it to me as thanks for all the lessons I paid for when he was 10 years old. I am a hundred and twenty plus duffer. So, you are not a student, Mr. Bernardi. At least not one of mine. How may I help you?"

"By telling me everything you know about your ex-wife Constance and her niece, Amanda."

"And why would I wish to do that?"

"Because Amanda has been murdered and the police are anxious to find out who is responsible."

He stares at me for the longest time. If he is surprised he does a good job of disguising it.

"You are not with the police."

"No," I say.

"Then what is your interest?"

"Personal."

"You were involved with her?"

"No. Not in that way. Not in any way in fact. It's a long story."

"I'm not going anywhere, Mr. Bernardi. Tell me your long story."

He leans back in his chair, lacing his fingers behind his neck, continuing to stare at me intently. I tell him the long story.

"Poor child," he says when I have finished. "A terrible way to die. I liked Amanda. I truly did, maybe because she was the free spirit that I never was, even in my teens."

"Can you think of anyone who might have wished to kill her?"

"No."

"In August she would have turned 21 and inherited millions. Now the money goes to your ex-wife."

His eyes narrow. "If that is an accusation, Mr. Bernardi, it is monstrous. Constance may be many things. She is not a murderess."

"Perhaps not. Tell me, what were the terms of your divorce?"

Mae was right. This is a soft spoken gentle man but now I see anger in his eyes. "That, too, is monstrous, Mr. Bernardi. Our divorce was quick and final with no strings. She has her life, I have mine. I doubt I've spoken to her more than once or twice in the past six months. And now if you don't mind, I'm busy. Goodbye, sir."

"Sorry to have bothered you," I say heading for the door. I open it and turn back. His glasses are once again perched on his nose and his head is down, engrossed in his paperwork. "Amanda's death is not yet public knowledge, Professor. The authorities would like to keep it that way as long as possible."

He doesn't respond, merely waves me away without looking up. I leave and trudge back to my car which is still parked in the administration lot. I start to open my car door, then reconsider. I walk inside. The helpful young lady is stapling some papers but is otherwise not engaged. She smiles at me.

"Did you find him?" she asks.

"I did, thank you," I say. "A matter of curiosity. I'm thinking of moving to this area and I will be looking for work. I'm a college professor with two published books and I wonder if you might have a position open starting in September."

"What field, sir?"

"Mathematics."

"Masters or PhD?"

"PhD."

"I know we are always looking for good people, especially doctorates but our Mr. Philby is who you want to speak to. He's not here right now."

"Not a problem. I can always stop back. Could you give me some idea of what a position here might pay?"

"Oh, I wouldn't know for sure," she says, "but with those qualifications I think it's around nine thousand, maybe a tad more."

I nod with a smile.

"Well, thank you. You've been a big help. I'll stop back tomorrow or the next day."

I slip behind the wheel of my car and now I have more questions than answers. I know that a teacher friend of Bunny's earns about $7300 a year at the local high school. She has a B.A. from a nondescript teacher's college. Professor Perry with his gilt-edged credentials is not making a great deal more, certainly not what he could earn at Stanford or some other prestige university. And yet, meager income or not, he doesn't seem to be hurting for money unless, of course, he is paying off his Cadillac over ten years which I seriously doubt.

I start the engine and drive to the main road and start to turn left. Lost in my thoughts, I pay little attention to the Forest Green Lincoln town car that is pulling in as I am pulling out. I don't really notice that a hefty, liveried chauffeur is behind the wheel and that he is alone in the car.

# CHAPTER SEVEN

I'm frozen in time. I was about to swing onto Route 101 north to return to Bodega Bay. Instead I pull to the side of the road and stare thoughtfully into space. With Bunny and Yvette back in L.A. by now, I have no reason to return to the hotel and in truth, I have more to do here in Palo Alto. Constance Perry is at the top of my list, provided I can somehow wriggle my way around her beefy chauffeur. And I'm not quite through with Roy Perry who seems to have a money tree growing in his backyard. No, returning to Bodega Bay is just a waste of time, gas and energy. I turn around and head for the center of Palo Alto.

The Burgundy Inn is an upscale motel with reasonable prices and a decent looking coffee shop. They also hand out toothbrushes, toothpaste and disposable razors for luggage-less travelers who pay in advance. I had dropped by the local branch of my L.A. bank and cashed a counter check for a couple of hundred dollars, then walked down the street to a men's store where I picked up a clean shirt, socks and underwear and a light sweater. Even in May this area gets chilly when the sun goes down.

The room looks comfortable but I stay only long enough to deposit my purchases and then head out for dinner. It's just past six and I have a plan but I'll need to kill a couple of hours before I can put it into effect. The coffee shop is featuring a meat loaf special which turns out to be very good. My waitress is very young and her name is Angela. She keeps refilling my coffee cup without complaint as I wait for eight o'clock to roll around. When it does I hand her a five buck tip on a six buck meal and ask where I can find The Pig Sty. As I suspected, she knew right where it was.

The sun has gone down and the temperature has dropped. Wisely I am wearing my new sweater underneath my sport jacket. It helps but not a lot. The Pig Sty, set back from the street on the edge of town, doesn't look like much from the outside. One story, wood framing, neon glowing in every available inch of window space. I pull into the parking lot which is far from full and find an isolated spot a ways from the entrance. I have a thing about parking lot dings and dents. They send me into a rage. I go inside. It's not much of an improvement on the exterior. I pull up a stool at the bar and survey the place. There's a decent sized dance floor and a Wurlitzer against the far wall is playing 'Blue Velvet' by Bobby Vinton. Four young couples are slow dancing and a few of the tables are occupied by dedicated boozers. In a far corner I see a bunch of guys, also young, shooting pool on two tables. Only quarter past eight and already a couple of them are obviously feeling no pain.

"What'll you have?"

I turn and look into the humorless face of the potbellied bartender.

"Coors in a glass," I say.

He grunts and walks away.

Two couples come in the front door laughing at some joke I missed. They yell at a couple at a far table. Whoops of laughter. Catcalls. Bobby Vinton disappears and some guy I've never heard before fills the room with 'Walk Like a Man." The bartender returns with my beer.

"If you're looking for action, buddy, you came to the wrong

place. These are mostly high school kids, maybe a few from the college."

"I'm a music lover," I say as some babe with unreliable tonsils starts to sing about a candy girl.

"Funny," the guy says dead pan.

"Actually, I'm looking for some information," I say as I pull an Andy Jackson from my wallet.

"What are you doing, writing a book?" he asks.

"Funny," I dead pan back at him. He actually smiles. "I want to pay for my beer and if I can get a little help with my research, I don't care about my change."

"I'm listening."

"Amanda Broome."

He nods. "I knew her. She moved away a couple of years ago."

"I'm told you had to eighty-six her a couple of times," I say.

"More than a couple."

"Couldn't hold her booze?"

He eyes me suspiciously. "What makes you think I served her booze?" he asks.

"A birdie told me and I'm not a cop."

He relaxes. If I say I'm not a cop and I am, he skates on all charges. It's how the game is played. I pose no threat.

"It wasn't just the booze. The babe was loud and foul-mouthed and thought she was queen of the ball."

"Not well-liked," I venture.

"Not much."

"Slept around?"

"Some," the bartender says, "but she was choosy."

"A heartbreaker?"

"Prick tease."

"I was trying to be polite," I say. "Anybody special?"

He hesitates thoughtfully, then looks over toward the pool

tables. "Guy in the blue sweater, looks like he needs a haircut. Jocko Pitts. She busted his balls real good. Whether he was actually getting any, I couldn't tell you."

The place is starting to fill up now and turning noisy. The candy girl babe disappears and real music starts to fill the room. 'Surfin' USA'. The Beach Boys. I hand the barkeep the twenty and leave my stool, taking my Coors with me as I wander over to the pool area.

Right away I must have looked like a pigeon. One of the kids smiles and politely asks me if I'm looking for a game.

I smile and shrug.

"For how much?"

"Five bucks."

"Nine ball?" I ask.

"Why not?"

I jab a finger in Jocko Pitts direction.

"I'll play him."

I get a smile. In fact all four of them smile. Jocko's smile is the broadest. I think I have just chosen the hustler-in-chief.

He steps forward. I extend my hand.

"Joe."

"Jocko."

He lays a fin on the rail. I follow suit. He chalks his cue.

"Lag for break?" he asks.

I shake my head. "Your option," I say generously.

"Thanks," he grins, signaling one of his pals who racks the balls tightly.

If I were breaking, they wouldn't be racked that tight at all. I'm really no pool player. I dabbled overseas during the war but it's been a long time since I've had a cue in my hand. Anyway, it makes no difference. I'm not here to beat this guy, I'm here to chat.

Jocko slams into the cue ball and scatters the nine balls helter-skelter and the seven drops in a side pocket. He smiles. He has a dead bang shot on the one and if he's any kind of player he'll have a cinch shot on the two.

"Jocko," I muse as he's lining up. "Jocko Pitts?"

"That's me," he says, slamming the one into the corner pocket and placing the cue ball close behind the two, inches from a side pocket.

"I ran into Amanda a couple of days ago," I say.

"Who?"

"Amanda Broome. She sends regards," I say offhandedly.

"What'd she do that for?" he asks as he pockets the two and goes in search of the three ball.

"Old times, I guess. I told her I was going to Palo Alto on business. Maybe she misses you."

"Maybe so. Wouldn't be surprised," Jocko says. He has no shot so he plays position leaving me without a shot as well. I try to look like I know what I'm doing, hit a clunker and accidentally skin the six ball.

"Oops," I say. "Out of practice."

"No problem," he says. Of course there's no problem. Now he has a clear shot at the three ball.

"I think she really feels bad about breaking it off with you," I say pleasantly.

He looks at me with a quirky smile.

"Her break up with me? You've got that all wrong, mister. Other way around. Ask the fellas. They'll tell you."

I look around. They're nodding in unison. I laugh.

"The bitch lied to me."

"It's her hobby," Jocko says, nailing the three with a decent set-up for the four.

"So you got tired of her, right?" I say,

"Bored stiff. She was a lousy lay but she always had a few bucks in her pocket."

"So you dump her. Some other guy moves in."

"There was no other guy. She was poison. Everybody knew it."

One of the other guys pipes up.

"Go on, Jocko. Tell him."

"Shut up," Jocko snaps.

This other guy looks at me with a grin.

"He won't tell you. I will. He got paid off."

"Stuff it, Snake," Jocko says with a growl and a dirty look. Snake is not intimidated.

"Guy comes in here. Big guy. Coulda been a wrestler. He hands Jocko a fat envelope loaded with tens and twenties. Five hundred bucks. Leave the girl be, he says. If you don't, next time you see me I'll break your fuckin' legs."

Jocko's in a rage, He shoots and misses. My turn.

"You talk too fuckin' much, Snake," Jocko says.

"Sorry, Jocko, my mistake." I say. "I was under the impression she'd broken your heart."

"In her dreams, that cunt," he replies.

"Any idea who the big guy was, Jocko?"

"Sure, the old lady's trained goon."

"The old lady?"

"Yeah, her aunt. Snooty bitch. The guy was her handyman, chauffeur, bodyguard. Frederick. Some kind of foreigner. Probably boffing her brains out every night."

I nod and take a careless shot at the four ball. I graze it, It goes nowhere near a pocket but it strikes the eight ball which hits the six ball which taps the nine ball into a side pocket. Suddenly and accidentally I have won the game. I can't believe it. Neither can Jocko.

"Jesus Christ," he mutters.

"Sorry," I say.

"Rematch," he glowers.

"Can't. Gotta go. But let me buy you guys another round of beer."

I pick up the near empty pitcher and wave it at the bartender. He nods in understanding. I put the pitcher down atop the two fives. Snake and the others grin. Even Jocko nods, half smiling. I put my hand in his shoulder and squeeze.

"You were right to take the money," I whisper.

And then I'm gone.

I exit the Pig Sty. It's now even chillier and I can't wait to get in the car and turn on the heater, My watch reads 9:02. I've just spent a very enlightening hour. Not that I know what it all means, I don't, but I think I'm getting a little closer to finding out who killed Amanda Broome. Maybe she was a selfish privileged bitch, I didn't know her, but I do know that 20 year old girls are not supposed to die like that.

I take out my keys and start to unlock the car when something slams into me. My head hits the roof, my knees buckle and I fall to the ground. A man's foot steps on my head, pressing down.

"Go back where you come from. You are not wanted here." a voice says. It's heavily accented. European, Maybe German. I squirm. The shoe presses down even harder. "The next time I see you the experience will not be so pleasant. Do you understand me?" I stop wriggling. "Do you?" I manage to grunt something.

"Hey!" a voice rings out. The shoe is lifted from my head. "What're you doing?"

I turn my head. A big guy in a Stanford sweatshirt is hurrying toward me. I turn the other way and, no surprise, Frederick the chauffeur is moving away quickly in the other direction. I watch as he slips behind the wheel of the green Town Car and drives off. Only then do I struggle to my feet as the big guy reaches my side. I can see he's young, probably a student, burly, with thinning reddish hair and sideburns.

"You okay. man?" he asks.

"Yeah. Fine. Thanks. Guy was after my wallet," I say.

"Sumbitch," my Stanford savior mumbles as the Town Car disappears around a corner.

I thank him again and shake his hand, assuring him that I am all right, and then I'm behind the wheel and on the way out of there, now a more enlightened man. I have spooked Constance enough to have King Kong sicced on me. More progress. Also more pain.

I'm back at the motel by nine-thirty. Still a decent hour. I phone my good friend Mick Clausen at home. Mick is a very successful L.A. bail bondsman with a big staff. There was a time when he would work till midnight, go home, open up again at seven in the morning. Then he met and married my ex-wife Lydia who quickly domesticated him. These days he's home for supper by eight o'clock and doesn't go back to the office until noon. His minions carry on in his stead.

Little Joe, his oldest kid and named for me, answers the phone. For a thirteen year old he's pleasant and outgoing and speaks in complete sentences. I love the guy and after we chat for a few moments, he puts his Dad on the phone.

"Is this social or otherwise?" Mick asks.

"Otherwise," I say.

"Thought so. Bunny told us about the babe in the trunk. Joe, you've got to start associating with a better class of people."

"Very funny, considering the social status of your average clientele."

"I'll ignore that," he says. "What kind of trouble are you in and how can I help?"

"I've run afoul of a gargantuan Kraut, former SS, I'm sure. I need to know all about him before he sends me to the hospital or worse."

"I'm taking notes. Shoot."

I pass on his name, who he works for, his address, a complete description including the ugly scar on his neck below his left ear. Yes, he has a driver's license so he's probably here legally. Mick says he has enough to go on. He'll get right on it.

"Joe, I know better than to tell you to leave it alone."

"I can't, Mick."

"You want me to send someone to watch your back? I've got a couple of guys just sitting around."

"Thanks but I'll be all right. If things get sticky, I'll call you back."

"See that you do," he says.

He hangs up. I set the alarm for eight a.m. I need an early start but I'm still not sure which approach will be the most productive. I climb into bed in my skivvies and turn on the television set. Paul Henreid is just lighting two cigarettes and handing one to Bette Davis. Oh, boy, 'Now Voyager', one of my favorite all time films and I haven't seen it in ages. This is going to be fun.

Six minutes later I'm sound asleep.

# CHAPTER EIGHT

The alarm shatters a great dream about me and Bunny on a beach in the south of France where covering, no matter how scanty, is considered superfluous. I glance at the clock. 7:15. Then I remember that last evening some damned fool set the clock for an early wake up to make the most of the day. Grumbling inwardly, I get to my feet, brush my teeth and splash a lot of water on my face. I dress in yesterday's wardrobe and head for the coffee shop. Angela is not on duty but Cissy May from Biloxi, Mississippi, does just fine. The coffee's hot and the eggs are perfect. By 8:20 I'm back in my room and on the phone to Ezra Crabtree at his home in Santa Rosa.

"I've been checking the television news. I presume no news is good news," I say.

"Holding steady," Ezra says. "Harry Felcher went out to Bodega to ask a lot of questions and fell getting out of his car. He tells it differently but either way he wasn't seriously hurt. Minor cuts and bruises."

"Good to know. What do you hear from the coroner?"

"Autopsy showed what you'd expect. Death by knife wound. Blood alcohol content very high. Also traces of cannabis. Sounds like the girl was partying before things turned sour."

"Time of death?"

"One a.m. give or take an hour. Before you ask, Rod was in his room alone and asleep."

"They know where she was killed?"

"Nope. Could have been anywhere. Killer drives her into the parking lot. It's deserted. Out of one car trunk into another and a quick goodbye. How are you doing?"

"I'll heal."

"Ran into a little trouble, did you?"

"Nothing that stiffer immigration laws couldn't cure. How's Rod doing?"

"Worried but hard at work. Henrietta has one of her people on the set keeping a watchful eye. I talked to what's his name, Deming, the chief honcho, and he says the company is returning to Los Angeles sometime next week. Not good for Rod. They may not let him leave the jurisdiction."

"Then we'd better get busy," I say.

"Guess we should," Ezra says and hangs up.

Now I have a choice. I can go bug Constance Perry or I can bug her ex, Roy, the affluent school teacher. Going after Constance doesn't seem promising if she is going to barricade herself behind wrought iron fencing. Besides I'm waiting for information about Frederick, her bully boy. No, Roy Perry is much more accessible but aside from Foothill College, I don't know where to find him. Being Saturday it is highly unlikely he will be in his office but I decide to give it a go anyway.

I was right. His office is locked and empty. In fact the entire building is pretty deserted. Unwilling to give in easily, I trudge over to the administration building. Wonder of wonders, young and helpful Georgia is once again on duty. I tell her my problem. She's sorry. Home addresses are confidential. I say it involves his medication. Loudly and sternly she says she cannot help me. Regulations are regulations. She has no choice. Then she whispers quietly, "He's in the book."

"Eh?"

"The phone book. He's in the phone book," she again whispers. I squeeze her hand and slink toward the door feeling every inch the dumb lout that I am. I find a phone book and my favorite garage owner gives me terrific directions to the Perry address in Los Altos Hills. I find it with ease. It's a beautifully kept up ranch on a half-acre. It's also the smallest house on the block but what a block! I park on the street and when I exit my car wafting in the air is the aroma of roses and honeysuckle and money. Lots of money. More curious than ever I stride to the front door and ring the bell. No response. I try knocking. Nothing. No one home. I check around the side. A new MGB roadster painted British racing green is parked at the head of the driveway. I peer into the living room window. All is quiet. I decide to wait, at least for a little while, and return to my car.

I don't wait long. Five minutes later the white Caddy pulls up behind me. I check the time. It's not yet ten o'clock. I get out of the car as Perry exits the driver side. A good looking young man gets out on the passenger side.

"Mr. Bernardi, back to visit so soon?" Perry asks, smiling.

"Couldn't stay away. This must be Hank."

"It is, just returned from Waco."

"Hi," I say.

"Hi," he says back, opening the trunk and taking out an over-nighter and an imposing set of golf clubs.

"Reunion golf tournament for alums from past Baylor golf teams. Don't ask how he did," Perry says.

"Fourth," Hank says. "Just out of the hardware."

"Better luck next time," I say. We shake hands. "Joe Bernardi."

"Nice to meet you, Mr. Bernardi. Like to stay and chat but I promised some of the guys I'd meet them at the club."

"Sure thing."

"Dinner in or out tonight, Dad?"

Perry checks his watch.

"Meet you in the Men's Grill at six o'clock."

"Grab my bag?" he says laying the overnighter on the walkway.

"Got it"

"Thanks. Nice meeting you, Mr. Bernardi," Hank says as he hurries off in the direction of that MGB in the driveway."

"Same here," I call after him.

Perry picks up his son's bag and we start up the walkway to the front door. We hear a vroom-vroom and then watch as the sports car backs out of the driveway. Hank waves goodbye and disappears down the street.

We go inside and Perry drops the bag in the foyer.

"Can I offer you something, Mr. Bernardi?"

"No. No thanks."

"You sure? I hate drinking alone."

"In that case, I'll have a beer."

"Coors all right?"

"You read my mind."

We walk out to a brick patio which is just off the living room. Nearby is a good-sized pool. The lawn is a deep green and the property is rimmed with flowers of every description. I must have been gawking because he says, "I have a very good gardener."

"Seems so," I say,

We sit down at a nearby circular umbrella table. He sips what looks like a gin and tonic. I take a deep pull on my beer.

"Hank has all the tools to be a top tier golfer," Perry says, "maybe even a successful pro like Palmer or Nicklaus. The tools but not the drive. No fire in the belly. I know we are not supposed to live our lives through our children but his lack of ambition is my only real heartache."

"He's a member of the Los Altos Hills Country Club."

"As am I. Actually he's a junior member but he's so valuable in the interclub matches that he enjoys all the privileges."

I nod.

"Did you tell him about Amanda?"

"You asked me not to. I didn't but now I believe I will. They grew up together. He has a right to know."

I shrug. "Why not? It'll come out any day now. It has to. The press will be all over the movie company like locusts and Rod Taylor will be tried and found guilty by a bloodthirsty press that thrives on scandal."

"Mr. Taylor. Yes, your friend, the actor. The man you claim is being framed."

"Not a claim, Professor. A certainty and trust me, I am going to get to the bottom of this."

Perry nods and again sips his drink.

"So, Mr. Bernardi, why are we meeting so soon again? Has there been a development or perhaps something you forgot to ask me."

I take another pull of my beer, gathering my thoughts.

"At the risk of appearing rude, Professor, I must ask you a frank question and I would appreciate a frank answer. Since I am not the police you needn't answer if you prefer not to."

"Ask away," he says.

"I have a pretty good idea of what you earn at the college. My question is, how can you afford this life style— the house, the car, the country club—"

He grins broadly, almost laughing.

"Yes, of course, I see. Never occurred to me. I don't think about the money that much. I'm an investor, Mr. Bernardi. Stock market. Have been for years. It's only in the last six or seven years that I've begun spending what I've earned. In the beginning it was to give Hank all the advantages. Golf lessons, a good schooling, four years at Baylor, the country club."

"You must be some kind of genius, Professor. Every stock I've ever bought turned out to be a dog. Who's your broker?"

"He's got an office in San Jose."

"What's his name?"

He gives me a sharp look.

"Why are you asking?"

"Just curious."

He shakes his head.

"Sorry but I'd just as soon not share Ed with anyone else. You understand."

"Your call," I say with a shrug.

"Funny," he says. "Me belonging to a country club. Never was a part of my life's ambition. Only did it for Hank. Sure I enjoy the camaraderie but basically I wanted my boy to every advantage that I never had. He's my best friend, you know."

"Unusual," I say.

"Very," he says. "But not unheard of."

"Then let me ask you this. Why Foothill College when Stanford is right around the corner?"

"A fair question. I'd just earned my PhD and had already published my first book. A prestigious eastern University made me an offer—never mind which one, they're all alike— and I signed on. I lasted a year. The snobbery and the socializing and the politics were suffocating me. I couldn't wait to escape. That's when I came west with Hank leaving behind my wife Claudia Brewster of the Back Bay Brewsters who divorced me before I was halfway across the country. I reasoned that Stanford would be no different than the Ivy League and when Foothill made me an offer, I took it, a decision I've never had reason to regret. I teach class in a turtleneck sweater and I can't remember the last time I had to take tea with the Dean at his residence."

"And then you remarried,"

His face darkens.

"Yes, in haste and not wisely."

"Followed by yet another divorce."

He shakes his head, almost amused.

"Yes, but this time it was my idea. The lady was too much for me to handle, too demanding with absolutely no sense of humor. Besides Hank hated her. Funny. A six old kid with the instincts of Dear Abby. I finally realized I was better off without her."

We talk like that for another thirty minutes in which he refreshes his drink twice. Maybe it's the booze, maybe not, but he chats easily and frankly about his life then and now, his solid relationship with his son and his joy of teaching at a school that didn't second guess his work habits. He looks me in the eye and no subject is off-limits and yet—and yet, I have a deep rooted feeling that I am not being told the truth, the whole truth and nothing but the truth.

It's shortly before noon when I leave having refused his offer of lunch. I want to get back to my hotel room in case Mick has called with information about Constance Perry's chauffeur-bodyguard, the ill-mannered Frederick. I turn onto Page Mill Road and start through the heart of town and then suddenly, out of the corner of my eye, I spot it in a municipal parking lot. The green Lincoln town car. I swerve instinctively into a metered curbside parking spot and cut the engine. I get out and look around for some sign of the lady or, more judiciously, her pet behemoth. No sign of either. As a precaution, I reach back into the glove box and extract my .25 Beretta and slip it into my trouser pocket. I don't expect to use it— I'm in the middle of a posh area of the town— but I have learned that I am always better off expecting the worst of my fellow man.

I walk halfway down the block, eyes searching everywhere and that's when I spot her emerging from a storefront office. The gilt lettering on the plate glass picture window reads "Isobel Graham,

Attorney at Law". Constance Perry is headed straight for the parking lot. No sign of Frederick. I jog across the street in order to intercept her.

"Mrs. Perry! Wait up!" I call out.

She turns toward me and her eyes widen in surprise, then narrow into little slits of annoyance.

"Mr. Bernardi, I thought I made it clear I am not interested in talking to you."

"Yeah, you did hint around a little but I was sure you didn't mean it."

"Oh, but I did."

I smile and fall into step beside her. "And me with so many questions and you with so many answers."

"Please leave me be, sir, or you can deal with the police."

"All I want is a few minutes of your time and your refusal to talk to me speaks volumes, Mrs. Perry, so if you feel compelled to bring the police into this, please do so."

"That may not be necessary," she says, her expression changing as she looks straight ahead. I follow her eyes. Frederick is just emerging from a hardware store carrying a small brown paper bag. His look latches onto mine. Anger shows on his face as I stop walking. Constance doesn't. Frederick starts toward me. There are a few people around but the street and sidewalks are far from crowded. I back up a couple of steps, reaching in my pocket, my hand clenching my pistol. Constance reaches him. He says something to her. She nods and keeps going toward the parking lot. I continue to back up. Frederick continues to advance. I produce the gun. He sees it, hesitates only for a moment and smiles broadly. He knows I'm not going to shoot him. His respect for me as an adversary is zilch. My only option now is to turn and run like a playground coward. Or is it? I spot a blue and white Palo Alto police cruiser coming down the street toward us. I stop backing away and when

Frederick is within a couple of feet of me, I raise the gun and fire three shots into the air.

Pedestrians scream in terror. Cars lurch to a halt. People scramble for cover. Frederick freezes in his tracks, then looks as the police car stops in mid-street and two officers climb out, drawing their weapons. With one final glare in my direction, he turns and darts down a nearby alley. I drop to my knees, spreadeagle myself in the sidewalk and shove the gun away.

"He threatened to kill me!" I scream like a baby. It's humiliating but I want that animal caught and cuffed and how it happens I don't care. The younger of the two cops, slim and athletic, takes off after Frederick. The other one, graying and sporting a well-nurtured beer belly, stands over me, gun pointed at my head, and says "Don't fucking move, asshole!"

Mike Hammer in a blue uniform. I don't fucking move.

# CHAPTER NINE

Thirty minutes later we are all comfortably gathered in the office of Palo Alto's Chief of Police, Alonzo Aaron Bridger. Well, not all. Me, the Chief, Constance Perry and the two cops. Frederick is among the missing. The lithe and athletic young officer who gave pursuit caught up with him several blocks away. Unfortunately Frederick was waiting for him and when the youngster appeared around a corner, Frederick felled him with one shot to the jaw, knocking him cold and absconding with his service revolver. Where Frederick is at the moment is not known but an APB has been broadcast by the Santa Clara Sheriff's Department. He has been described as armed and dangerous in the hopes that some law enforcement officer will blow him away on sight. Cops get testy when perps steal their weaponry. Frederick is in deep doo-doo unless he loses himself within the bowels of Oakland where the citizenry would happily hide Jack the Ripper if the Bobbies were after him.

"I assume you have a permit for this thing," Chief Bridger asks me laconically, fondling my prized Beretta. He's middle aged, sandy-haired and smokes a pipe. This may be the most exciting day he's had in a month. I reach in my wallet for my carry permit and hand it over. He gives it a cursory look and hands them back, gun and permit both. He has already wormed out of me that I am a published author and screenwriter and that for the past few days I have been staying at Bodega Bay during the filming of Alfred Hitchcock's new film. If this impresses him, he shows no sign of it.

"May I go now?" I ask.

"Not yet. What was the shooting all about?" he asks.

I tell him, dwelling on Frederick's attack on my person at the Pig Sty and the threats of more to come. "I fired the gun into the air only to attract the attention of your officers."

"And why would the man attack you?" Chief Bridger asks.

"Because I was trying to ask questions of Mrs. Perry."

"About what?"

"I can't tell you that."

"Oh, you can't, eh? Well, hereabouts, Mr. Bernardi, we do not go around asking questions of Miz Perry. She is one of our leading citizens and we treat her with the deference that she deserves."

"Then I'd say you have a problem on your hands, Chief," I say, "since the only one here who knows the remotest thing about your fugitive is Mrs. Perry and she seems to be off-limits to any type of inquiry."

Bridger gives me a flinty look and it is a warning. Here is a man who does not like to be challenged and who will not let any slight go undealt with. I look toward Constance who gives me the dirtiest of looks before she turns to the Chief.

"I would be happy to answer any questions you might have about Frederick, Chief, although frankly I know little about him."

"Thank you, Miz Perry. How long has the man been working for you?"

"I hired him about three months ago. He responded to an ad my private secretary had placed in the Santa Rosa Press Democrat for a handyman-chauffeur."

"His last name?"

"Schurling."

"And he had references?"

"No. He had worked for several years for a man in Napa who had recently died. His son, with whom Frederick did not get along, fired him and refused a decent reference. After spending an hour with the man, I was persuaded he could perform the duties that were required of him and I hired him."

"And those duties were?"

"General handyman, chauffeur and bodyguard."

Bridger nods slowly. "All right, you may go, Miz Perry, and thank you again for your cooperation."

Constance gets to her feet. "Happy to help," she says and heads for the door. I also stand up.

"I think I'll be going as well, Chief," I say.

"Sit down, Mr. Bernardi."

"I don't think so," I say, "unless you're ready to arrest me in which case I will call Ezra Crabtree in Santa Rosa to come down here and bail me out."

I thought I noticed a slight paling of the skin when I mentioned Ezra's name.

"Where are you staying?" he asks.

"At the Burgundy Inn, at least for tonight. If my plans change, I'll let you know."

Bridger hesitates, then grunts and waves me away. I don't wait for a second grunt but at the open doorway I turn back.

"Just a suggestion, Chief, but if I were you I'd have a fingerprint guy go over Mrs. Perry's car. Your runaway perp may just be in the system."

"Thanks for the advice, Mr. Bernardi, and next time you have trouble writing one of your books, call me and I'll see what I can do for you."

He smiles. I smile back and then I'm out on the street, searching for the departing figure of Constance Perry. I spot her on the opposite sidewalk looking a little bewildered. I jog across the street to her side.

"May I help you, Mrs. Perry? You seem lost," I say.

"Trying to decide the best way to get home, Mr. Bernardi. Frederick locked the car."

"And you don't have a spare key?"

"No, and if I did, it would make no difference. I do not drive."

"You don't drive at all?"

"Never learned. Never wanted to."

"How about if I take you home, Mrs. Perry, and you can arrange for someone to pick up your car tomorrow."

"No, thank you," she snaps.

"Look, Mrs. Perry, I'm trying to be civil about this but sooner or later you are going to have to answer some tough questions, if not to me then to the police." She looks at me, puzzled. "Ma'am your niece has just been brutally murdered only a scant few weeks before she would have inherited millions of dollars, money that will now go to you."

She glares at me. "What you are suggesting is monstrous."

"Yet there it is," I say, "and when the press gets wind of it, your name will be splashed across the front page of every cheap tabloid in the country. First the brutal murder of your brother some years ago, now the even bloodier demise of your niece, Amanda Broome, both deaths resulting in a sudden uptick in your fortunes and providing you a life style you never could have imagined."

"Untrue!" she gasps.

"Maybe so but truth is seldom an ingredient in tabloid sensationalism."

She hesitates for a moment.

"Very well, Mr. Bernardi, you may drive me home and I will answer your questions the best I can but if you think I am responsible for Amanda's death your are seriously mistaken."

As we head out of town, I drive cautiously and query her casually. How did she and Amanda get along? How difficult was it raising a headstrong privileged young girl? Did she have many friends? Male? Female? Did she bring them to the house? What school did she attend? Public or private? How were her studies? She responds calmly but everything screams that this woman must be responsible for Amanda's murder although it's highly unlikely she personally committed the deed. Frederick comes to mind, particularly when she is quick to give me her alibi for the time of Amanda's death.

"I spent the evening with Isobel," she says.

"Isobel Graham, your lawyer."

"That's right. We had an early dinner together at an Italian restaurant and then went back to her place."

"What time did you leave?"

"I didn't."

"You spent the entire night going over legal documents?"

"Hardly."

"Then your relationship is something more than attorney-client."

"Yes and has been for many years, Mr. Bernardi. I am 50 years old. I had one short-lived marriage which convinced me that I had little interest in the male of the species. I'm sure Roy must have told you all about it."

"No," I say, "in fact, he merely said the two of you were incompatible and left it at that."

She smiles sardonically. "Yes, in some things, Roy can be quite the gentleman."

"Frederick. Where did he sleep?" I ask. She looks at me curiously. "He drove you to town. He had to stay somewhere. A guest room?"

"I took a cab to town. The next morning Isobel drove me home."

"And where was Frederick?"

"I don't know. He said he needed the evening off. I gave it to him."

"Any idea what he was up to?"

"None."

If you're one of those conspiracy theorists, here is your murderess deadbang. Motive, means and opportunity by proxy. It's so neat I have trouble believing it and the chief reason for my doubt is Rod Taylor. As Rod said, someone is going to a lot of trouble to hang a frame around him. Constance Perry? If so, why? It makes no sense.

At that moment, I pull up to the iron gates that guard her driveway. Constance grabs her door handle.

"I'll walk the rest of the way," she says, starting to exit the car.

"That's a long walk to the house. I'll drive you."

She smiles mirthlessly, leaning toward me. "I'd just as soon you didn't."

She walks toward the gate, a remote device in her hand. The gates swing open and she walks through. A quick glance back and then she starts up the drive as the gates close behind her.

It's close to five o'clock when I return to the Burgundy Inn. I have one message and it's from Mick Clausen.

"Has this character waved a gun at you, Joe?" Mick asks.

"Not yet."

"Well, he will. His name is Frederick Schurling. He came here in 1950 as a refugee from East Germany. Three years ago he was released from Tehachapi after serving four years for aggravated assault and attempted murder."

"Lovely," I say.

"You might want to clue in the cops if they don't already know."

"The guy's in the wind, Mick, after assaulting a police officer and stealing his service revolver. A statewide APB has been issued."

"Excellent. You sure you don't want one of my boys up there to help out?"

"Thanks anyway, Mick, but right now I'm the least of his problems. Hi to Lydia. Tell her I'm fine."

"Will do."

I hang up and start for the bathroom. I manage three steps before the phone rings. I answer it.

"Mr. Bernardi, Peggy Robertson. I have Mr. Hitchcock for you."

A moment later Hitch comes on the line.

"Joseph, dear boy, I hate to interrupt your amateur sleuthing but you are needed desperately here at Bodega Bay."

"What's going on, Hitch?"

"The veil of silence has been ripped asunder. A couple of hours ago, a local television station broke the news of Mr. Taylor's predicament. As I speak reporters are appearing from far and wide, camping outside the hotel, pulling people aside, taking photos and generally making pests of themselves. Someone has got to deal with them and it is certainly not going to be me."

"I'm in Palo Alto, Hitch, getting ready to come back. I shouldn't be much more than an hour at the most."

"Do hurry. I'm counting on you." And with that he hangs up.

I check out of my room and swing by police headquarters where I pass on to the Chief what I learned from Mick. I tell him I'm returning to Bodega Bay and give him the number of the hotel where I can be reached. He grudgingly permits me to leave and a few minutes later I'm heading north toward the Golden Gate Bridge. I stay with Route 1 after leaving the bridge. It's not dark yet but the sun is setting out over the ocean. By the time I turn onto Valley Ford, a country road that meanders through the mountains toward the coast, I am traveling intermittently through bright light and deep shadows. For the first time I notice the car in back of me. It looks like a Buick, maybe an Olds, and it's hovering back about ten lengths although it could easily pass me any time it wanted.

A road sign looms up on my right. 'Slow Speed. Dangerous

Curves Ahead.' They aren't kidding. I drive into a couple of switchbacks, reach a summit and then start down. More sharp curves and then suddenly the trailing car is upon me and slamming into the rear of my Bentley. I look in my rear view and try to identify the driver but the glare of the sun on his windshield thwarts me. Slam. Slam. He comes up beside me on my left and tries to shove me off the road, attempting to force me through a guard rail on my right into the ravine below. I see a hooded figure at the wheel but I can't make out his face. I fight the wheel, trying not to skid out. I come to a turn and there in front of me on my left is a relatively flat piece of land guarded by a split rail fence. Beyond are a dozen newly mown haystacks. I hit the brakes and the Olds flies ahead of me. I yank the wheel left and crash through the flimsy fence heading straight for a haystack, simultaneously hitting the brakes. I come to a dead stop, covered with hay, reach in the glove box for my pistol and open my door, rolling out onto the ground and landing hard on my left shoulder as pain shoots down my arm. I look back toward the road. The other car, a late model two-toned Olds 88 is sitting quietly, idling. I take dead aim on the driver's side window and pull the trigger three times in quick succession. Glass shatters. I think I may have hit him but then I watch as the driver guns the engine and pulls out onto the road, speeding away and disappearing around the next curve.

I get to my feet and brush away the hay atop the car, then climb back in and turn the key. The engine starts and I slip into first gear. Grudgingly the car moves forward. I turn and head back to the road. The engine is making weird hissing sounds and the chassis seems to be wobbling. Maybe a flat. Maybe a misalignment. I stop and clear away the shattered remnants of the split rail fence, then drive out onto the shoulder of the road. I check the tires. They seem okay but the engine is still hissing and now I hear a periodic clicking noise.

I slip behind the wheel and pull out onto the road. All is well until I reach 20 miles an hour and then the car starts to shudder and buck. I ease off, crawling toward Bodega Bay in the distance, my trusty Beretta laying on the passenger seat beside me. I am taking no chances.

# CHAPTER TEN

It's a few minutes past seven when I hiss and ping my way into Bodega Bay and struggle up the hill to the hotel which suddenly looks like a thriving enterprise. The parking lot is nearly full, every window on the main floor is lit up and raucous laughter is emanating from the bar. A couple of Sheriff's cruisers sit in the shadows off to the side of the building and two trucks sporting TV station call letters are parked by the front door hogging six parking spots. America's free press is here in force, ready to do its duty to keep the public informed no matter how salacious the subject matter. I find a parking spot a hundred yards from the entrance, grab my pistol and gingerly exit my car. My left shoulder is throbbing but the pain has abated and my arm feels almost normal. I move my head from side to side with little discomfort but my left knee continues to feel violated by sharp little knives. I limp toward the main entrance and, grasping the railing, climb the three steps to the front porch and go inside.

As advertised the bar is jammed as is the lounge area. I spot Peggy Robertson behind the reception desk talking to the manager and elbow my way toward her. She sees me coming and an expression of relief crosses her face.

"Joe! Where have you been? We've been worried about you," she says.

"It's a long story," I reply. "Where's Rod?"

"In his room."

"How is he?"

"What you'd expect. Nervous, angry, maybe a little scared."

"And Hitch?"

"Back in San Francisco by now."

"You're in charge," I say.

"Lucky me," she smiles.

Just then I spot Sergeant Hayes emerging from the men's room at the end of the corridor, wringing his wet hands dry. I wave to him and he makes a beeline in my direction.

"You should have been here an hour ago," he says.

"I was held up," I say and then tell him about my adventure out on Valley Ford Road. His expression darkens as does Peggy's.

"What nest of rattlesnakes did you stir up down there in Palo Alto?" he asks.

"God knows," I reply.

"And you're pretty sure the car was a late model Oldsmobile?"

"One or two years old at most. Two toned, teal blue and white, an 88. Last week my neighbor bought one just like it for his wife."

"I'll put it out on the radio. Maybe we'll get lucky. You get a look at the guy?"

"No, he was wearing one of those sweat shirts with a hood but I'm pretty sure I know who was driving," I say. I tell him about Frederick Shurling and what I learned from Mick. "There's an APB out on him issued by the Palo Alto police."

Hayes nods. "I'll check the wire," he says. "Meanwhile I'd like to clear these people out of here. Some of them are turning into nasty drunks and I don't have the authority to boot them. Any ideas?"

I nod. "Leave them to me." I squeeze Peggy's hand and make my way into the bar. The noise level rises several decibels. I grab a chair and with great difficulty, climb upon it.

"Ladies and gentlemen," I say loudly to no effect. I look around. I try a different tack. "All of you, shut the hell up!" I scream at the top of my lungs. A few people fall silent, some turn to look at me. "Quiet!" I shout again and a moment later the room falls silent. I look around making sure I have everyone's attention.

"My name is Joe Bernardi and I represent the film company and I am here to tell you that you're not only wasting your time, you are disrupting the guests at this hotel. There is nothing you are going to learn here this evening." I hear grumbling coming from my left and I whip my head in that direction and stare down the loudmouth. He falls quiet.

"Tomorrow morning at nine o'clock I am going to hold a press conference at the Tides down by the wharf. Those of you who leave now quietly and without complaint will be welcome. In thirty minutes I am going to scour the premises. Any reporter still remaining will be barred from tomorrow's proceedings." I hear a low level rumbling starting up. "Barred!" I emphasize. "No exceptions. Any questions?"

"Will Mr. Taylor be available for questions?"

"Yes," I say emphatically. "Anything else?"

One guy pipes up. "Is it true that the woman was Taylor's fiance?"

I glare at the dense knucklehead. "For the benefit of your deaf compatriot and others with trouble comprehending the English language, I will repeat myself. The Tides. Tomorrow morning. Nine o'clock. Now all of you, get the hell out of here!"

They grumble but they go. Fifteen minutes later the place is dead quiet and devoid of the press. Joe Bernardi, exterminator extraordinaire. Peggy thanks me. Sergeant Hayes thanks me. The manager, whose name is Leo Brickell, has just seen a congregation of well-heeled lushes exit the premises like the rats leaving Hamelin. He does not thank me. He is a sweaty little man with a face like a ferret and I don't really care what he thinks. I tell him I am tired and hungry. He tells me to go to bed, that the kitchen is closed. I remind him that the kitchen doesn't close until nine-thirty. He tells me that tonight the kitchen closes at eleven minutes to nine. Sergeant Hayes smiles. Excellent news, he says. Since the kitchen won't be serving meals, it's an ideal time for a comprehensive county health inspection. Brickell blanches and decides to reverse himself. I thank him and ask for a cheeseburger with chips and a cold Coors be delivered to my room while I go upstairs to confer with Mr. Taylor. Brickell is more than delighted to cooperate.

I knock softly on Rod's door.

"Rod, it's me. Joe."

"Door's open, mate," I hear him say.

I step inside. He's standing by the window looking down on the near deserted parking lot, a can of beer in his hand.

"They scattered pretty fast," he said. "You threaten them?"

"Absolutely. I told them, leave or I shut you out of tomorrow's press briefing."

"Which briefing is that?"

"The one I said you'd be attending at nine o'clock tomorrow morning. Of course you won't be. Not possible on advice of counsel but I have a statement here from Mr. Taylor which I will read to you. Ms. Broome was a casual acquaintance. Hadn't seen her in weeks. No clue as to why her body would have been planted in the trunk of my car. Blah, blah, blah. Any further questions, direct them to my attorney, Ezra Crabtree."

"What about mentioning the restraining order?"

"Forget it. That only invites a lot more questions that you don't want to deal with. So, Rod, just how much did you know about Amanda?"

"Aside from the fact that she seemed to have a screw loose, not much," he replies draining his beer and tossing the can in a nearby trash basket. "So what do you say, Joe, shall we crack another tinnie?"

"What?"

"Sorry, I keep forgetting you people don't speak proper English. I asked if you'd like a can of beer."

"I've got one waiting in my room where I'll be off to in about ten minutes. Meantime, let me tell you all about the obnoxious Miss Broome." With that I proceed to tell him everything I learned about Amanda and her family and her acquaintances in Palo Alto. He listens intently and when I'm finished he slumps down into an easy chair, shaking his head.

"Christ, I knew she was away with the pixies."

"What?"

"Sorry again, mate. Away with the pixies. You know, balmy," Rod says. "Not right in the head. She kept saying she'd be worth millions, that she'd buy me a studio so I could play any part in any movie I wanted. I thought she was daft."

"Well, she wasn't. In August she would have come into upwards of twenty million dollars."

"Poor kid. So who gets the money and don't tell me the wicked stepfather."

"Actually, it's the wicked aunt," I say.

He shakes his head in disbelief. "No. I've seen that movie or one like it a dozen times. I think I was even in one."

"Nonetheless—" I leave it unsaid.

He goes to the minibar and takes out a cold can of Budweiser.

"I suppose the old lady could have done it. Or had someone do it for her. Like the chauffeur. But what's it got to do with me?" He looks at me, bewildered.

"No clue, Rod." I check my watch and get to my feet. "And now I am going off to my room, totally nackered."

He grins broadly. "Now you're learning, chum."

"I do a lot of crossword puzzles," I say opening the door.

"Joe." I hesitate in the doorway. "Tomorrow morning. The briefing. I'll be there."

"Not a good idea, Rod," I warn him.

"It'll look worse if they get the idea I'm hiding in my room. I can handle these guys."

I shake my head. "I believe Davy Crockett said the very same thing at the Alamo."

Rod opens his fresh beer.

"I'll meet you in the lobby at twenty to nine tomorrow morning. Night, Joe. Sleep tight."

I hesitate, then realize argument is futile. I walk out, closing the door behind me and head for the staircase and my room, one flight up. Some people believe they are blessed with superpowers which will help them overcome any situation. Others have to stick a hand into the flame before they are convinced it is hot. Unless he is very adroit or very lucky, tomorrow morning Rod Taylor will come face to face with reality in the form of a free press. Experience tells me it will not be pretty.

My cheeseburger is cold and my beer is warm but I try not to notice as I call home. Bunny answers, relieved to hear that I am alive and then becoming testy when she realizes we haven't talked since I left her at the airport. I tell her what I've been up to, leaving out my ugly confrontation with Frederick the 'Grate' and the unfortunate episode on the road back to the hotel. She wants to know when I will be returning home. I tell her I don't know. Soon, I hope. I plant a phone-kiss on her and hang up, then call Ezra at his home.

"Is he out of his mind?" Ezra asks after I tell him that Rod is going to play pinata for the press tomorrow morning. We agree it's a lousy idea but Rod is probably thinking of his he-man image. Innocent men do not hide in hotel rooms. If his next room has bars in the window, he may wish he'd reconsidered such a foolhardy position. Ezra promises to be on hand in the morning and hangs up. I force down the burger and the beer as I check the news broadcasts on the television set. Rod's face flashes on-screen followed by a smiling photo of Amanda in her high school prom dress. Henrietta Boyle and Sergeant Hayes are interviewed. They say very little of substance and wisely deny that Rod is a suspect, merely one of many people being queried.

I flip off the TV, hobble into the bathroom and toss down four aspirin, then return to the easy chair by the window and sit in the dark, contemplating tomorrow morning. The contemplating makes me wish I were back in Los Angeles once again flakking B movies for Jack Warner.

It's eight-thirty five the next morning when I exit the elevator into the lobby. Rod is waiting by the front entrance and tells me all about the scrumptious breakfast he'd had delivered to his room. I don't tell him that I had breakfasted on salted peanuts, a Three Musketeers bar and a can of Budweiser. My hobbling has improved to a limp and we walk briskly across the parking lot toward my car. Rod has written out a statement. I really don't want to read it but I know I must. I'm relieved to discover it is short, concise, and sticks to the facts. Good. The real challenge will come in fending off questions like "Did she scream a lot when you dragged her into your car? A simple yes or no will do, Mr. Taylor."

Wheezing and pinging, the Bentley gets us to the Tides by five to nine. Since it's Sunday the company's not shooting and a dozen or more crew members are hanging around outside, curious about developments. I spot Jessica Tandy and her husband, Hume Cronyn, sitting at an outside table drinking coffee with Suzanne Pleshette. Norm Deming, the unit manager, is pacing nervously while puffing on a cigar. Inside, the place is crowded, every table and chair accounted for, and owner Mitch Zankitch and his staff are doling out free danish and coffee to everyone in sight hoping it will pay off with a mention in whatever news stories are filed. Gracie James and her camera are flitting here and there, snapping everything in sight. If she's lucky a fight will break out and she'll have something to sell to one of the papers. I spot Evan Hunter at a table in the corner. He's grinning and I can imagine what he's thinking: excrement about to hit the fan. Ezra Crabtree appears out of nowhere and leads me to a makeshift podium set atop the counter.

"This is lunacy," the lawyer says out of the corner of his mouth.

"This is show business," I respond in kind.

I quiet everyone down and then prepare to turn the floor over to Rod.

"Mr. Taylor will read a short statement and then is prepared to answer your questions. Most of you know that I am not employed by the movie company, that I am overseeing this press conference as a favor to Mr. Taylor and Mr. Hitchcock. A warning. In your zeal to file your stories, ladies and gentlemen, take particular care to get your facts straight and to avoid slanting things for the sake of sensationalism. I know the folks at MCA-Universal and they are hard-nosed and unforgiving. You will be able to cross them once and only once and for the sake of your future paychecks, heed my advice. Play this straight."

I step aside to give Rod the podium. He smiles, oozing charm and reads his statement with sincerity. He constantly makes eye contact and his audience is silent, soaking in every word and for a brief moment I think he is going to get away with this. Then comes the first question from a weasly guy up front wearing horn rims and a bow tie.

"How long were you dating this eighteen year old girl, Mr. Taylor?"

"A few weeks," Rod says, "and she had told me she was twenty-six."

"And you had broken off the relationship when?" comes a

different voice from the back of the room.

"About six months ago. I thought it was amicable. I was wrong. Almost immediately the harassment began. Letters. Phone calls, some at three in the morning. I would find her waiting outside my apartment house. She started bothering my friends. Finally I had to take out a restraining order."

"You must have been furious," a voice calls out.

"Annoyed, yes. Furious, no. By then I realized she was just a kid, a misguided fan. I felt sorry for her."

"Even when she showed up at your hotel a few nights ago? I understand there was a fight in the lobby."

"Not a fight. We had words. I threatened to call the police. She left."

Another voice. Reporters are starting to talk at once now.

"Was that before or after you contemplated killing her?"

"That's absurd. I never—"

"You were overheard at dinner saying you'd be happy to run her over with a truck," a woman shouts out.

"That was a joke," Rod shouts back testily.

"The woman's dead. That's no joke," someone shouts out.

"Belt up, you bloody ghoul!" Rod shouts back.

Another voice from the rear of the room.

"What does your fiancee think of all this, Mr. Taylor?"

Rod turns red with anger.

"Leave her out of this!"

"Is she standing by you, sir?"

"Just where is your fiancee, Mr. Taylor? How much had you told her about your secret love affair with Amanda Broome?"

Ezra steps forward, ready to elbow Rod out of the way and take the mike, but just at that moment, the front door of the restaurant bursts open and Henrietta Boyle sweeps in, flanked by two burly Sheriff's deputies.

"Sorry, people, party's over," she says loudly, making a beeline in our direction. "Mr. Taylor, please accompany me outside."

I shoot a look at Ezra. Normally he'd be screaming about high handed police tactics but Henrietta has just rescued his client from an embarrassing inquisition. He grabs Rod by the elbow and tells him to play along.

"You folks stay put and finish your coffee," Henrietta says to the crowd. "I'll be available for your questions later today."

And with that, we exit the Tides, Rod squeezed between the two deputies, Henrietta in the lead and Ezra and I tagging along behind. We make our way to the far end of the wharf where a dark blue unmarked Chrysler is parked. One of the deputies lags behind to discourage curiosity seekers as we reach the Chrysler and relative privacy.

"Is my client under arrest, Miz Boyle?"

"Not yet, Counselor. But I have questions." She turns to Rod. "Forensics went over your car thoroughly, Mr. Taylor."

"I'm sure they did," he replies.

"On the floor under the driver's seat they found a ticket for a car wash dated eight days ago. Full wash and wax and detailing."

"I take good care of my car. What's your point?"

"I believe you told us that, aside from the other night at the hotel, you hadn't seen Amanda Broome in at least a month."

"That's right."

"Then maybe you could explain to my satisfaction what Miss Broome's fingerprints were doing all over the interior of your car."

Henrietta Boyle stares him down without flinching.

# CHAPTER ELEVEN

Rod seems totally flummoxed. He screws up his face in confusion, lost for the moment without an answer.

"Well," Henrietta says, "shall I repeat the question?"

"No, no," he says. "It's just that—No, wait. I just remembered."

Henrietta fixes him with a beady stare.

"Mr. Taylor, you have no idea how thrilled I am when a suspect in a criminal investigation looks at me and suddenly blurts out,' Wait, I just remembered'."

"It was a week ago," Rod says. "The day before I drove up here. I'd been having lunch at Musso's with a producer named Jerry Kaplan. Mr. Bernardi knows him. I'm going to do their next movie. Lunch is over. The valet brings my car. I get in behind the wheel and suddenly the passenger door opens and Amanda climbs into the car. She wants to talk and tries to put her arms around me. I tell her to get out and try to push her away. She won't leave. Chris, the parking valet, sees what's happening and helps me fight her off. She's screaming a blue streak, cursing me up and down and everybody is staring and then Chris has her out onto the sidewalk and kicks the door shut. When he waves me away, I take off."

"I'll assume this Chris will back up your story," Henrietta says.

"Of course he will," Rod says.

"Satisfied, Henrietta?" Ezra asks.

"I may be after I talk to this Chris person. Even so it doesn't prove Mr. Taylor's innocence."

"No? Then why don't you explain the scratch marks on the trunk lock of Mr. Taylor's car," Ezra says.

She glares at him.

"Who have you been talking to?" she demands to know.

"Henrietta, your department has more leaks than the Titanic. As you well know, your forensics people believe the lock was jimmied which seems to rule out Mr. Taylor."

"Not entirely," she says, "but it's the chief reason I haven't yet made an arrest. However, Ezra, I'm told the movie company will be returning to Los Angeles at the end of the week and if so and in the absence of any further developments, I intend to hold Mr. Taylor here in Sonoma County as a material witness."

"You won't hold him long, Henrietta," Ezra says.

"We'll see."

"May I presume that we are now free to go?"

"For the moment, yes, but keep your client available."

She climbs into the backseat of the Chrysler and a minute later, she and her police escort are headed back to Santa Rosa.

"Not sure I like the way she's mucking around," Rod says.

"She's bluffing," I say.

"Maybe so but she's playing silly buggers with my life," Rod says grimly.

"I wouldn't worry," says Ezra. "She knows better than to go up against Universal Studios and risk a multi-million dollar lawsuit against the county. If she hasn't got enough to arrest you, Rod, she'll let you go, at least temporarily."

"I feel so much better," Rod says wryly.

Ezra, who was up at six o'clock and hasn't yet eaten, invites Rod and me to join him for a proper breakfast in the hotel dining room. I demur politely. I have loose ends that need to be tied and so I leave the two of them and head for my room where I place a call to my producer Jerry Kaplan. By now the story's out and I need to bring Jerry up to speed. No, I don't think it likely that our star will be doing twenty to life for murder when he's supposed to be playing the lead in my screenplay but Jerry is a worrier who sees disaster peeking around every corner. It's my job to pacify him, no mean task. After forty-five minutes of cajoling and schmoozing I have Jerry throttled down from wild-eyed panic to jittery nerves and an upset stomach. I promise to stay in touch.

Sergeant Hayes is next on my list. I call the Sheriff's Department in Santa Rosa to get his home phone and am surprised to learn he is working, even though it's Sunday. I'm even more surprised by what he has to tell me.

"The Olds 88 was stolen off a Palo Alto street mid-afternoon on Saturday, the theft reported around five o'clock. The owner, a Mrs. O'Banion admits to leaving the keys in the car. Then around ten-thirty that evening one of our cruisers reports in. The car is back in Palo Alto, abandoned in a vacant lot about a block from where it was originally parked at Alma and Hope."

"Weird," I say.

"There's no question it was the car that came after you. There were dings and dents and paint marks on the right side of the car and the driver's side window was shattered by gunfire."

"You check for prints?"

"There were none. It had been wiped clean."

"Frederick?"

"Maybe. The Chief tells me he's got someone out near the Broome place in case Schurling shows up. He thinks the guy may be something more to the old lady than just a handyman."

"My thoughts exactly. Keep me posted," I say.

"I'll do that," Hayes replies and hangs up.

I call down to the front desk and ask for Norman Deming's room number but when I dial it the line is busy. I hang up, try again. Same problem. I leave my room and climb the stairs to the third floor where I knock on the door to 308.

"Yeah? Come in," the production manager's voice growls from within. I open the door and pop my head in. Deming is at the writing desk, papers strewn in front of him, talking on the phone. He waves me in and I flop down in his easy chair. Remnants of toast and coffee are sitting on a room service tray by the door and Norman Deming is not in a good mood.

"Yes, sir, I get that you have nineteen years experience but are you union?... Sir, I'm sorry but you could be Ben Franklin himself and if you don't have a union card, I can't use you. Could you tell me if anyone in the area— Hello? Sir? Mr. Lang?" He stares at the hand piece and then slams it down on the cradle.

"Not a good day," I observe.

"You hire these locals in good faith and they stick around for three for four days and then they just disappear. Making movies is not quite as glamorous as they thought it would be. So far I've lost a backup electrician, a standby painter, a Teamster and two laborers and I need replacements by tomorrow morning." He holds up a slip of paper. "This guy had to leave for Denver to be his cousin's best man at a city hall wedding. I got another guy broke his finger laying dolly track. He's going to apply for workman's comp. This other guy I can't even find. Put his address down as the old folks retirement home at the edge of town. Patrick Hannigan, unskilled laborer. Nobody there ever heard of the guy and I owe him a hundred and fifty bucks for three days work. Well, fuck him and fuck his hundred and fifty bucks. Hey, you wanna help dig a trench tomorrow, Joe? Fifty bucks and lunch. Best deal in town."

"No thanks."

"Good thinking. Now what is it I can do for you?"

"I hear you're moving back to L.A. this coming week."

"Not at this rate we're not," Deming says, relighting an ugly cigar that has been sitting cold in a nearby ashtray. "What's your problem?"

"You might be going back without your star."

"Christ, that's all I need," he growls, shaking his head.

"I'm working on the problem, Norm, but I need as much time as you can give me," I say.

"My schedule board says we move Friday but we could spill into Saturday. That won't cost me my job. If we're still here a week from now I'm gonna hear about it." He looks over at me with a wan smile. "Get the guy out of trouble, will you, Joe? My gut hasn't got room for another ulcer."

I leave Norman to his misery and return to my room. Sergeant Hayes is turning out to be an ally and a smart cop. Boyle is political through and through and being very cautious. Shutting down a multimillion dollar movie will almost certainly do nothing for her career. On the other hand nailing a well-known actor for a brutal murder will turn her into a celebrity and clear the way for any job she goes after, maybe even Governor. I have got to turn her head in the direction of Constance Perry and her pet gorilla because there are certain maxims in police biz. Wife dies, take a hard look at the husband. Businessman dies, check and double check the partner. And above all this watchword, when in doubt, follow the money and in this case, the money leads directly to Constance Perry's formidable iron gates. I think to myself, all I need is time to move the spotlight away from Rod but time is the one thing I don't have.

An hour passes. Being Sunday, there's not a lot I can do even if I had a clue as to what that would be. I check the shooting schedule for the coming week. Exteriors Monday through Friday including a major scene in the schoolyard where the children are attacked by the birds and the subsequent sequence where they race down the street in search of cover. I'm told this involves tricky setups and could spill over into the following day. I hope this is the case but if not, and all goes well, travel to L.A. will take place on Saturday. Then, too, rain could bollix things up and I find myself staring out my window at a blue and cloudless sky. No rain in sight and none expected. Damn.

Finally I come to grips with my only real alternative. Had I been able to identify Frederick as the driver of the Oldsmobile, Rod would be freed of suspicion. Obviously I have to make myself available for another try and the best way to do this is to poke a stick at the nest of vipers as obnoxiously as I can. Even I can recognize that this entails a certain amount of risk so I pick up the phone and call Mick Clausen.

"I've changed my mind. I need help," I tell him when he comes on the line.

"First smart thing I've heard you say since 'I do' at your wedding," he says. "What's the latest?"

I fill him in on developments to date, reiterating my confrontation with Frederick in the Pig Sty parking lot as well as the recent game of car tag in the winding hills above Bodega Bay.

"Jesus, Joe, how much doo-doo can you step in without getting yourself killed? I'm beginning to think you have a death wish."

"Enough with the sermonizing, Mick. Will you help or not?"

"I'll have somebody there by eight this evening. Use an outside phone to book a room under the name Harry Longabaugh. Don't make public contact. Better that no one knows he's there to back you up."

"Harry Longabaugh," I say. "Who the hell is Harry Longabaugh?"

"Better known as The Sundance Kid. Meantime, do nothing, my friend, and I mean nothing. Professional help is on the way and all you can do is screw things up worse than you already have."

"But—"

It's the only word I got out. Mick had hung up. I follow suit and check my watch. Nearly two o'clock. Hours to kill. Nothing to do. I decide to go out to the pool area and grab some sunshine while putting away a brew or two but when I step outside I notice a brisk breeze in the air. I look up. The sky is no longer a virgin blue and grey water-laden clouds are drifting into view.

"No!" I rail to myself. "Not today. Not Sunday. Tomorrow!"

The rain holds off and I fall asleep on a chaise at poolside, waking up around five thirty, very very hungry. I wander into the hotel coffee shop in search of a sandwich and find Evan Hunter at a table in the corner, eating alone, sipping red wine and reading a book. He spots me and waves me over. I pull up the chair opposite him and throw a quick glance at his paperback, 'The Girl Hunters'.

"Mickey Spillane," I observe.

"A dandy writer who sees things in black and white. Helps me keep my 87th Precinct books on an even keel. Of course, when some Nosy Nellie asks what I'm reading these days I usually reply Proust or Hesse."

"Of course," I say, being someone who also reads for fun, not because someone thinks it's good for me. "Us troglodytes have got to stick together."

A waiter comes by and I order a chicken salad sandwich on rye and a Coors. As he leaves, Evan leans back and eyes me curiously.

"Well," he says, "I understand you've been a busy boy."

"Too busy," I reply. "I'm going to have to cut back."

"But you're still in one piece, thank the Lord for that. So what do you think, Joe? Do you think this picture will actually get made?"

"Sure."

"With or without Rod Taylor? Or for that matter, with or without Evan Hunter?"

"That's an odd thing to say."

He shrugs. "For weeks Hitch and I have been struggling to find a decent ending for this picture. I finally came up with one but I'm pretty sure he isn't going to shoot it. Even if he does, I doubt he'll use it."

"Tell me," I say.

"Sure. The birds have been in attack mode for hours. They're everywhere, then suddenly turn quiet. They sit watching and waiting. The power's out everywhere. No radio reports. No one knows how widespread this terror extends but Mitch realizes they can't stay in Bodega Bay so everyone bundles into his car, the convertible, and they start off. Suddenly the birds start to swarm again. They attack the car, beaks start to rip through the flimsy top, the women start to scream in horror as the birds shred the canvas and then just as suddenly as they started, they stop and lag behind. San Francisco lies ahead. But, the viewer may wonder, what lies in wait in San Francisco? Safety or more avian madness? Fade out. Finis. End credits."

"I love it," I tell him, smiling broadly.

"Hitch doesn't. Too melodramatic, too pat, too Hollywood. He's got it in his head that he's creating something important, something for the critics."

"You're kidding."

"Wish I was. He's still looking for his first Oscar. Pappy Ford's looking for number five. Hitch wants respect and in my opinion he'll do what it takes to get it."

"Sad."

"Yeah." He downs a swig of wine as my beer and sandwich arrive.

Seven-thirty rolls around and I camp out in the lobby with a mug of coffee. I want to see who Mick sent. Most of his guys I know by sight and I'm hoping it's Kim Waites. Kim's one of Mick's female 'guys', tough, bright and fearless. Exactly what I need for my plan of action. It's ten of eight when he rolls in except it isn't Kim, it's Mick.

This is even better except I am going to pay dearly for dragging Mick into this personally. His wife, Lydia (my ex), and my loving wife Bunny are fast friends and when they compare notes (and they WILL compare notes) my name is going to be mired in four letter words, some of which I haven't used since I was in eighth grade.

He's carrying a small overnight bag and our eyes meet only fleetingly as he checks in at the desk. He signs the register, then puts his hand behind his back and flashes a signal. Two fingers, one finger, two fingers. I watch as he gets into the elevator for the second floor. I wait for a minute or two, finish my coffee and then get up and head for the stairwell.

I knock gently at 212. A moment later he opens the door, drags me in by my shirt front and quickly shuts the door.

"I wanted you to phone. You could have been seen," he snaps.

"I wasn't."

"But you could have been."

"I was careful."

"You're always careful and most times you come within a whisker of getting yourself killed."

"No one saw me," I protest

"We've been over that."

"I need a beer."

"Help yourself."

He flops down on the sofa and I grab a beer from the minibar, pop the cap and sit down in the easy chair. I take a deep swallow. Mick doesn't join me because he's a recovering alcoholic and has been for decades.

"Somebody's trying to kill me," I say.

"I gathered that," Mick says."Why?"

"I know something."

"What?"

"I have no idea."

"Who? That chauffeur?"

"Maybe."

"Okay, somebody's trying to kill you. You don't know why and you don't know who."

"That about sums it up."

"And your plan is?"

"To make myself available."

"The cheese in the trap."

"You bet."

Mick shakes his head. "Meanwhile I am supposed to protect you from this homicidal maniac whoever he or she is."

"Frederick."

"We don't know that for sure."

"But likely. Okay. Now tell me about this hare-brained scheme of yours."

"Patience, my friend," I say, as I go to his bedside phone and place a call to Ezra Crabtree.

# CHAPTER TWELVE

I really should have my car looked at but I haven't got the time. The next morning, shortly past nine o'clock I am wheezing my way toward Palo Alto. Mick is in his rental car a short distance behind, always in sight. I feel somewhat secure with my small caliber Beretta in my trouser pocket but Mick's the one with the enforcer, a snub-nosed .38 revolver which he carries in a holster nestled in the small of his back beneath his jacket.

I have not called ahead for an appointment because I don't want to risk my targets comparing notes and coming up with some bogus fairy tale. Once in the middle of town, I get lucky and find a parking spot three doors down from her law office. I feed a few dimes into the meter and watch as Mick pulls up across the street next to a fire hydrant. Since he won't be leaving his car, he runs no risk of getting a ticket.

Isobel Graham's pretty young receptionist whose name is Wanda, or so says her desk plaque, smiles up at me.

"Miss Graham, please," I say politely.

"Do you have an appointment, sir?"

"No, but you can tell her that I am about to file a hundred thousand dollar lawsuit against one of her clients." I hand her one of my precious 'Joseph Bernardi, Author' business cards. Wanda glances at it and if she's impressed, she does a good job of hiding it.

"One moment," she says and gets up from her desk. She raps softly on a nearby door and steps inside. A moment later she reappears. "Miss Graham will see you," she says.

Isobel Graham is about what I expected. Early to mid-forties, plain features with little makeup, short cropped brunette hair and wearing a navy blue jacket and skirt. Around her neck she wears a yellow bandana and when she comes around her desk to greet me, she does so with authority. Her handshake is firm and her smile is well practiced.

"Mr. Bernardi."

"Miss Graham."

"Please sit." She beckons to a nearby chair. "Normally I don't have time for drop-ins but a hundred thousand dollars caught my attention. What's this all about?" She returns to her desk and picks up a #2 Ticonderoga which she fiddles with, her eyes never leaving mine.

"Constance Perry, Palo Alto's newest multi-millionaire. I spent several days trying unsuccessfully to talk to her about the death of her niece, Amanda. Apparently she finally got annoyed by my persistence and sent an employee out to do me bodily harm of the worst kind.

"I doubt that," she says coolly.

"Doubt it all you like, Miss Graham, but papers will be filed tomorrow morning by my attorney, Ezra Crabtree." I had hoped for a reaction to Ezra's name and I got one.

"This employee, are we talking about Frederick Shurling?"

"You know we are."

"If true, this is the first I have heard of it. I will have to check with Mrs. Perry."

"Of course."

She looks me up and down, curious.

"You're not an attorney, Mr. Bernardi. What's your interest in all this?"

"I'm acting on behalf of a friend. I find all of this—" I grope for the word. "Bizarre."

"How so?"

"Thirteen years ago you were with Constance Perry when she arrived home and found her brother dead on the floor of the library."

"Yes, we'd been attending a meeting of the Literary Club. I drove her home. She doesn't drive. Never learned."

"So I understand. At the time she was divorced from Roy Perry. What was your relationship?"

"We were casual friends. Not that it's any of your business."

"But your relationship now is considerably more intimate." I can see a lie coming. I ward her off. "Don't bother to deny it, Miss Graham. Mrs. Perry has already admitted as much."

"Again, it's none of your business."

"I know but lying to me seems to be a popular sport around here and I'm getting both annoyed and suspicious. Suspicious. Yes, definitely suspicious. Thirteen years ago a robust man was shot to death, allegedly during the commission of a burglary. Several days ago a young woman was nearly decapitated and her body moved to implicate an innocent man. And what do I get for my queries? Half truths and prevarications. I'm being treated like a fool and I don't like it, Miss Graham, not one bit, so I am going to keep asking questions until I get to the truth."

She allows herself a faint smile. "Assuming that what you say is even partially true about Frederick, is there any way we can resolve this without going to court?"

"You might suggest Ms. Perry talk to me candidly about Amanda's death. That would help a lot."

She hesitates momentarily, then nods. "I'll see what I can do. Check back with me around noon." She gets to her feet. Meeting over. I also stand.

"I'll call you," I say. I reach in my wallet and take out another of my valuable business cards. I scribble on the back and hand it to her. "This is where you can reach me if I drive back to Bodega. If I stay in town, I'll be at the Burgundy Inn."

I walk toward the door, stop and turn back.

"Incidentally, I'm curious. Now that Mrs. Perry inherits the estate that would have gone to Amanda, just how much money is involved?"

"That's not really relevant," Isobel replies.

"And that, Miss Graham, is a one hundred thousand dollar non-answer." I stare her down.

"As I said, it's irrelevant but not a secret. It's in the neighborhood of twenty million dollars."

"Thank you," I smile. "I'll call you at noon."

I leave and head back to my car. Mick is still parked across the street by the hydrant. I give him a nod of the head. He nods back and I pull away from the curb and head for the outskirts of town. He follows. A few minutes later I spot an abandoned warehouse and drive to the rear of its rutted parking lot, barely visible from the road. Mick follows me. We cannot be seen from the road.

"How did it go?" he asks.

"Well," I say. "I think she's trying to set up a meeting."

He shrugs. "Okay, it's a start."

"Something else," I say. "I asked how much money Constance was coming into because of Amanda's demise. She said about twenty million."

"Nice piece of change."

"The old man set up the trust thirteen years ago with eighteen million dollars."

Mick looks at me in disbelief.

"That's crazy. By now the trust should be worth at least thirty million."

"A suspicious CPA might think that. Or even a kid who had just graduated first grade mathematics."

"So maybe Madame Executrix has been dipping into the till."

"Even granting the lady had excessive managerial fees, there is no maybe about it."

"And come August and Amanda's twenty-first birthday, the young lady might have wondered where all the money went."

"The thought crossed my mind, Mick," I say.

"The cops should find that interesting," Mick says.

"Maybe not. Constance Perry and her late brother are institutions in these parts. The authorities may not dig deeper than the topsoil if they bother to dig at all."

Mick gives me a grim look. All men are created equal. That phrase seems to have nothing to do with Constance Perry.

At noon I find a phone booth and call Isobel Graham. She comes on the line right away.

"I'm afraid I have disappointing news, Mr. Bernardi. Constance has no interest in talking to you."

"Then I guess we'll meet in court."

"Her words as well. I told her that I had already talked to your attorney, Mr. Crabtree, and warned her that he would be a formidable foe. She said she didn't care. In her view the lawsuit is trumped up nonsense, she is sure she will prevail and even if she doesn't, an adverse verdict will do little to dent her bank account. Sorry. I did my best."

"I'm sure you did, Miss Graham. We'll be seeing you."

I drive back to the warehouse where Mick has been waiting for my return. I recount my conversation with Isobel Graham. He shakes his head.

"The lady wants to play hardball," Mick says.

"She can afford it."

"So where does that leave us?"

116

"Empty handed, but before we leave town there's something I want to check out."

With a little help from some friendly pedestrians, I find my way to the intersection of Alma and Hope, Mick following discreetly behind. Alma Avenue is home to a couple of dozen store front businesses. A parking spot is open up ahead and I slip into it. I still have some loose change for the meter which will allow me the 90 minute max before I risk a ticket. Mick finds a spot at the end of the block near Hope. The vacant lot that Sergeant Hayes had told me about is about thirty yards in back of me, across the street.

I exit the Bentley. The Olds was stolen from this area Saturday afternoon and if I'm lucky, maybe, just maybe, someone saw something. The Bank of America is useless. Closed on Saturdays. I have higher hopes for Willie's Barber Shop and the Peninsula Deli two doors down. Meanwhile Mick is working the block from the other end.

Otto, the deli owner, is no help. Saturday is a busy day. He was working the meat counter non-stop from nine o'clock in the morning. He saw nothing, but I'm welcome to ask around. I do and strike out. I have slightly better luck with Willie, the barber.

"I remember the car. Blue and white. Very flashy," Willie says. "It was parked across the street, over there." He points.

"What time was this?"

"Lunchtime. Maybe a little later."

"You see anybody hanging around it?"

"Not particularly. You need a trim."

"What?"

"I could take a little off the back, straighten up by the ears."

"No. No thanks. So you didn't see it drive away."

"Naw, but it was gone by three. That's when I stepped outside for a cigarette. My customers don't like me stinking up the shop, thinks it's gonna give 'em cancer with the smoke and all."

"Don't suppose you saw the car return, park in that vacant lot over there."

"I close at six, mister. If the car came back, I never saw it. You sure about that trim?"

I leave a disappointed Willie behind as I continue down the street, Mick coming toward me. He exits a tobacco shop and subtly shakes his head. I respond in kind, then walk over to him and pantomime confusion, as if I am lost and need directions.

"You want to do a little surveillance work?" I ask him.

"Mmm, my favorite," he says with a grimace.

I tell him about Roy Perry, a poorly paid community college teacher and his puzzling life style which includes a membership in the Los Altos Hills Country Club, a man who supposedly has gotten rich in the stock market but refuses to tell me the name of his broker.

"Maybe I should poke around," Mick says.

"Couldn't hurt," I reply. "I'm going to stop by police headquarters and see if there's anything new on Frederick Shurling. Then I'll head back to Bodega."

"Fine, but stick to the main highways even if it takes a little longer. Do not drive any lightly traveled mountain roads."

"Yes, boss. I hear you, boss," I grin and then I jog across the street to my car.

I stop by police headquarters which is housed in an imposing looking building on Bryant Street. The Chief is out but his deputy tells me there's been no sighting yet of Frederick Shurling. They've asked the County Sheriff to expand the BOLO (Be on the Look Out ) to the eleven western states. I'm pretty sure he's not hanging around anywhere close but nevertheless I take Mick's advice and stick to the main roads back to Bodega. It's past two o'clock when I return and I find Rod out by the pool area with a very attractive woman who turns out to be his fiancee, the model Mary Hilem, here to show support. They are scheduled to be married within the next couple of weeks, God and Henrietta Boyle willing. The company is out on Bay Hill Road shooting Tippi as she drives her car to the town and barring anything unexpected, Rod is through for the day. I fill him in as optimistically as I can about developments, express congratulations on the upcoming nuptials and then head off for my room. I am exhausted and need at least an hour's worth of shuteye.

I'm awakened around five-thirty by my phone. I answer groggily. It's Mick.

"Order room service to be delivered at seven-thirty. Steak medium rare, baked potato, asparagus. We have a lot to talk about."

"Do I get to eat too?"

"Sure, order what you like."

"They'll think I have a woman in my room."

"Good. It'll make you sound more dashing and mysterious. Seven-thirty. I'm leaving now." He hangs up.

At seven-thirty sharp, there's a knock on my door. I open it to admit the room service waiter and his cart. He smiles in greeting and looks around, then transforms the cart into a table. Steak, baked potato, asparagus, rack of lamb, scalloped potatoes, steamed onions, a Caesar salad, two slices of chocolate cake and a large carafe of coffee. He presents me with the check and looks around again. The bathroom door is open. No one there. He smiles with one more glance at the food. 'Bon appetite', he says and leaves. A minute later there's a soft rap on the door. I open it and Mick slips inside. 'Mmm' he says, admiring our feast. 'Let's eat'.

We dig in as Mick starts to tell me about his afternoon.

"I spent about an hour wandering around the professor's neighborhood talking to anyone I could find outdoors. I'm moving to the area next month, I tell them, just checking out the real estate. The usual drill. Is it quiet? How are the neighbors? Any problems I should know about? I didn't learn much. Perry and his kid keep pretty much to themselves. No complaints. They're just an unknown quantity. I had better luck at the country club."

He slathers butter on his baked potato. I swear I can see his arteries bulge from the clogging. I shove my potatoes aside and dabble at my salad.

"Same story. I have a little six bedroom shack in Bel Air in Los Angeles. Hate to move but business brings me to Palo Alto. Need a proper challenge for my golf game. A guy named Humbert shows me around. Dining room, men's smoker, trophy room. Picture of Hank Perry on the wall holding a trophy. One of our younger members, Humbert tells me. We're very proud of him. Later I find out from one of the guys in the bag room that the kid is a real shit."

"Not the way his Dad tells it," I say.

"Should I be surprised? Hank's a pretty good golfer and scores even better with the ladies. A new one every few weeks. Even though he doesn't work he always seems to have money but he doesn't throw it around. That car of his, Daddy bought it for him new. When he signs a check he always uses his father's name and I was told that this past year he's gotten a couple of girls in trouble. That last part may just be a jealous rumor. Maybe not."

"And the father?"

"People like him. They call him Doc and treat him as an equal even though most of the members could probably buy and sell him ten times over."

"Maybe not our killer?" I suggest.

Mick shakes his head.

"I learned a long time ago not to jump to that conclusion. The evil among us come in all shapes and sizes, Joe, and they are adept at hiding it."

# CHAPTER THIRTEEN

Tuesday morning. My travel alarm tinkles in my ear. Seven-fifteen. I force myself into the bathroom, brush my teeth with the latest miracle dentifrice and gargle a capful of Listerine. Then I go to the phone and call home.

"Hello," comes Bunny's voice.

"Get off the phone, ma'am. I want to talk to the lady of the house," I growl.

"The lady of the house is just putting her book bag in order. She has nine minutes until her bus comes so talk fast."

"Hi, Daddy," Yvette says with a sparkle. "When are you coming home?"

"Pretty soon now, Princess. I miss you."

"I miss you too. Hobart has a toothache." Hobart is her pet turtle.

"I don't think turtles have teeth, honey," I say.

"Oh, yes," she says, "and it's very painful. After school we're going to take him to the doctor."

"In that case I guess he'll be fine."

Having exhausted the subject of Hobart's tooth, she tells me about her new pair of shoes, a new girl in class named Veronica who seems very nice and a substitute teacher who isn't. I listen with enthusiasm to her life, so filled with meaningful and exciting trivialities and try to think back to when I was ten. I can't or maybe I don't want to. I'm giving my daughter the childhood I never had and loving every minute of it. I think I hear a hurried goodbye and then Bunny comes on the phone.

"Lydia is ready to kill you," she hisses into the phone.

"Mick's fine. We're in no danger."

"Then what's he doing there?" she asks. "My God, Joe, the man's sixty-two. He should be home with his wife and kids."

"He said he was going to send someone else."

"He always says that and he always shows up himself."

"Bunny, I'm not his keeper."

"Well, he needs one. What's going on?"

I tell her as best I can knowing that it all adds up to a lot of nothing. We have maybe four or five days left before the company returns to the sound stages at Universal City. Rod is still on the hook though he hasn't been arrested. Not yet. Come Saturday, he may be.

"And you're safe," she says quietly.

"I'm safe," I reply.

"See that you are," she says. "Yvette would miss you."

She hangs up and I smile.

I get dressed and look down at the parking lot. A sheriff's cruiser sits by the front door and an officer is standing on the porch steps checking room keys. We can turn away nosy reporters but we can't bar paying guests and a few enterprising journalists with fat expense accounts have taken rooms in order to waylay Rod. So far none has succeeded.

The dining room is pretty empty. Mick is at a table alone against the far wall. He's reading the morning paper. He looks up, our eyes meet, he goes back to the paper. I grab a table near the kitchen. My waitress is named Myrtle, greying and grandmotherly. I order eggs, sausage, toast and coffee and sit back, wondering where I go from here. My trip to Palo Alto did not provoke another attack on my person. I tried to bully both Constance Perry and Isobel Graham and failed miserably on both counts. Mick learned that the professor was a neighborhood loner but well liked by his fellow club members and that his son was a spoiled brat, hardly a hanging offense. So what now? I've pretty much run out of ideas.

They arrive together, my breakfast from the kitchen and the clerk from the front desk who has an urgent call for me from Ezra Crabtree. I look longingly at my breakfast and then get up from the table and hurry into the lobby.

"This had better be good. My eggs are getting cold," I say.

"Better than good. They ran Frederick Shurling to ground."

"They have him in custody then."

"Not exactly. He slipped away at the last second. He's been staying in Half Moon Bay with a street corner hooker for an indeterminate amount of time. Apparently somebody recognized him from news broadcasts but when the cops showed he went out the back way."

"The hooker, what is she saying?" I ask.

"Nothing. Name's Olga Bergen. German probably. Maybe Danish. They're holding her on aiding and abetting."

"Perhaps we should talk to her. Can you shake loose?"

"I'm in court at ten. Shouldn't take long. Then I'm free. Meet you at police headquarters at noon."

"Right."

I hang up, encouraged that we may have gotten a break. I wander back into the dining room where Myrtle has covered my breakfast, keeping it warm. I decide it'll stay warm a few minutes longer and catch Mick's eye. I head nod in the direction of the Men's Room. He nods in understanding. I go first. A minute later he joins me. I've already checked the stalls for eavesdroppers. Quickly I fill him in on the situation.

"Good," he says. "I'll follow you down there."

"No," I say, "you're going home. I'm getting a lot of crap from Bunny who's getting it from Lydia."

"My wife is going to have to learn to stay out of my business," he grumbles.

"Be sure to tell her that when you get home," I say. "Look, Mick, I appreciate your help, I really do, but our boy Freddie is running from the cops. The last thing he's worried about is me. Believe me, I'll be fine."

We go back and forth but he digs in his heels. He'll stay at the hotel until I return with whatever Ezra and I can get out of the hooker. Then we'll revisit the subject of his return home.

Half Moon Bay is a sleepy little town on the ocean about fifteen miles west of Palo Alto. It boasts a chief of police, six deputies and a ramshackle headquarters building converted from a private home on the edge of town. I arrive at three minutes to noon, Ezra arrives at three minutes after. We enter in tandem in search of the chief who turns out to be an amiable roly-poly balding man who used to work as a night supervisor for a private security firm. Ezra introduces himself and passes me off as his associate. He says he is here to represent Olga Bergen.

The Chief, whose name is Hal, couldn't care less and leads us to a makeshift cell at the back of the building. "Holler when you're done," he says, unlocking the door. He ambles back to his private office, a converted bedroom with a view of the tire store next door.

"I did not ask for lawyer," Olga says. "I have no money to pay."

She is a sturdy woman, somewhere in middle age, with the visage of a loser. If you look hard enough you might see that at one time she was attractive but that was long ago. Her mouth droops down. It may be a permanent condition.

"No money is necessary, Olga. We've come to help," Ezra tells her. "We have a few questions for you and after that, we'll get you out of here."

"I do not answer questions from police," she says adamantly.

"I am not the police. Mr. Bernardi is not the police. Please help us and we will help you. Now, how long have you known Mr. Schurling?"

She hesitates, still wary, then says, "We are old friends. Many years. Back in Munich he was boxer. Very good but not much pay and dishonest manager so he gets into other work. Not so honest. Very dangerous. Police come for him. He get away, hide in boat, come to America. The next year I get visa. Two years ago he sees me on street in San Jose. I am happy. He is happy. After that he comes to see me maybe two or three times a month."

"He pays you," I say, trying to clarify this relationship.

She glares at me. "Yes, he pays me. Why not? He has plenty of money."

Ezra and I share a quick glance.

"He works as a chauffeur, Miss Bergen."

"Yes, for the nasty old lady."

"Not a job that pays a lot."

"No, but he takes. How do you say it, off the top?"

"The top of what?"

"The payments."

"What payments?" I ask.

"For the alimony, though Frederick thinks they may be for something else. I think yes, maybe he is right. Alimony is not paid like this."

I'm totally lost. So is Ezra.

"Maybe you'd better explain," Ezra says.

"Is simple. Once each month Frederick takes the money to the husband at his house."

"You mean Roy Perry, the ex-husband," I say.

"Yes, that is correct. Ex-husband. It is alimony payment, the old lady says. In the beginning, two thousand dollars."

"Each month?" Ezra says, almost disbelieving.

"Yes. Like I say, In the beginning was two thousand but Frederick, he knows these two they do not talk. Much hate. So he goes to old lady and says husband now wants twenty five hundred. To her this is small amount so she pays. Frederick gives two thousand to old husband, keeps five hundred dollars for himself."

Ezra and I share a look.

"Alimony," he mumbles in disbelief.

"In a pig's eye," I echo. But if not alimony, then what? Blackmail? Sure sounds like it.

"So the police are after him and Frederick needs a place to stay. He comes calling," I say. "Late Saturday evening? Nine or ten o'clock?"

"Earlier," she says. "Before supper."

"No," I say.

"I am making soup on the stove. The clock on the wall says five-thirty. I must eat and then go out to the streets to sell sex. Frederick comes to the door. He is very upset. I let him in."

"You're lying, Olga. It was later than that," I say. It has to be. At five-thirty I was being chased by a homicidal maniac in the hills above Bodega Bay.

"I do not lie. I know what I say. I do not make soup at ten o'clock at night." She fixes me with a hard stare. "Now maybe you get me out of this place."

I leave that up to Ezra and it isn't difficult. Olga has not been formally booked so when Ezra hands the Chief two hundred dollars in "bail money" he pockets the cash and sets her free. Once out in the parking lot I offer Olga a ride to her house but she says no, she will walk and maybe pick up some sex business on the way. Ezra hands her his card and tells her to call him if Frederick shows up again. If she does and he is captured, Ezra will see that she receives a five hundred dollar reward. She looks at the card, slips it into her cleavage and then walks out to the street, sticking out her thumb for the benefit of a passing motorist.

I look at Ezra.

"What do you think?" I ask.

"I think Constance Perry has a big time dirty secret shared only by her ex-husband," Ezra says.

"I think also we know the source of Roy Perry's wealth and it has nothing to do with some non-existent stock broker in San Jose."

"And that's not all," Ezra observes.

"I know. If Frederick was knocking on Olga's cottage door at five-thirty Saturday afternoon, then who the hell was chasing me all around the mountain roads above Bodega Bay at the exact same time?"

Ezra has no answer. Neither do I. I only know that this case has taken a sudden left turn into Nowheresville.

Ezra heads back to Santa Rosa. I make my way to Bodega Bay stopping once to make a phone call to Mick. He's not in his room so I leave a message. "Harry, my room. 4:00." I omit my name. Precisely at four, he knocks and I let him in and within ten minutes I have filled him in on everything that Ezra and I were able to extract from Olga.

"I'm staying," he says flatly.

"It wasn't Frederick that was trying to kill me," I protest.

"Obviously, but it was somebody, you idiot, somebody you don't know about which is even more dangerous, besides which, Frederick is still on the loose and maybe he's looking to step on your head again."

Grudgingly I pick up on his logic but if he stays, he's going to have to deal with his wife, not me. We make plans to return to Palo Alto the following morning to rattle a couple of cages. Since Constance Perry is cowering behind the gates of Fortress Broome, Isobel Graham is a more likely target as is Roy Perry, your friendly neighborhood blackmailer. I remember thinking the first time I talked to him that he wasn't showing all his cards. Olga's revelation puts him back near the top of my list.

That night I dine with Rod and Mary and I assure them that all that can be done is being done and the outlook is good for Rod's return to Los Angeles at the end of the week. I sometimes amaze myself by how easily I lie but it comes from years of experience as a publicity man. Any man who can thump the tub with a straight face for a Best Actor nomination for Tab Hunter in 'Battle Cry' is capable of just about anything. Despite his best efforts to hide it, I can see that Rod is worried and conversation is at times difficult, particularly because we have been joined by Jessica Tandy and her husband, Hume Cronyn, and by Evan Hunter who Mary was dying to meet. One of her all-time favorite films is 'The Blackboard Jungle'. Evan is annoyed because he is sure Hume is badmouthing his script changes to Hitchcock behind his back and subtle daggers fly between them while Jessica is furious with Hitch over the imperious way he is treating Tippi Hedren. The movie business. A world of its own. I can't wait until dessert is done with and I can escape to my room.

At last it's over, at least for me. The others have ordered brandy. I have passed and now I am in the lobby headed for the elevator when the manager, Leo Brickell, signals to me. A word in my office, he says to me, so I follow him into a cramped little cubbyhole behind the main desk. He sits. I sit. He clears his throat. I wait expectantly.

"We—that is, me, as well as staff—are immensely proud of our hotel and present ourselves in the best light possible, hoping that our guests will emulate our manners and good taste."

"Yes?"

"We feel, that is, I feel that what a person does in the privacy of his own home is his business and his alone but when certain behavior spills over into the public arena, I believe steps must be taken."

"Absolutely," I say, having no clue as to what he is talking about.

"Then you can appreciate my dismay at the behavior of you and Mr. Longabaugh in Room 212."

Aha, perversion raises its ugly head, I think to myself.

"Several times you have been observed sneaking into one another's rooms. This morning in the dining room you allowed your breakfast to get cold while you went into the men's room. A few moments later, Mr. Longabaugh joined you. You were in there quite a while, according to my sources."

"Ah, yes. Excellent. It's working then," I say.

"What? What's working?" Brickell asks, totally bewildered.

"Our cover."

"What cover?" Brickell asks.

I lean forward, my eyes sternly fixed on Brickell's.

"This goes no farther than this room."

"Yes, yes, of course."

"Certain distasteful elements from the East Coast are trying to worm their way into the industry's unions. Mr. Longabaugh— that's not his real name, by the way—is an undercover FBI agent working with Universal and the leadership of IATSE to ferret them out. I'm Mr. Longabaugh's handler. If his true identity were to be revealed it could be very dangerous."

"Yes, I see," says Brickell, wide-eyed.

"Say nothing of this to anyone," I tell him.

"I understand," he says.

I get up from my chair and stare down at him.

"Your government thanks you for your patriotism," I say and then turn and leave. On the way to the elevator I briefly contemplate the idea of opening an oceanfront hotel, once my mental faculties have turned to mush, the latter apparently being a requirement for such a venture.

# CHAPTER FOURTEEN

Wednesday morning. Mick and I tandem back to Palo Alto. My kidneys get a workout as the Bentley shimmies and shakes but at least I run no risk of getting a speeding ticket. It's a few minutes to ten when I pull up in front of Isobel Graham's law office. I feed the meter with some change I got from the hotel desk clerk, having now concluded that Palo Alto supports itself on nickels and dimes from it's profitable curbside bandits. Mick is contributing across the street.

I tell my old friend, Wanda, Isobel's receptionist, that I need to see the lady but am told I am out of luck. She's at the weekly brunch for the Friends of the Palo Alto Medical Clinic. Ms. Graham is chairman of the fundraising committee, Wanda brags somewhat snobbishly. I ask where this event is being held. She tells me. I know where it is. I ought to. I've passed by it enough times in the past several days. It's too far to walk so I drive over having wasted seventy-five cents in the damned parking meter. No doubt Mick is equally peeved.

The Merrick Hotel is an old fashioned eight story landmark that has seen better days. So has the valet who takes my car from me. I walk inside and locate the daily activities easel, then wend my way to the Fremont Room where I open the door a crack and peer in.

It's on the smallish side and most seats are taken. Isobel is sitting at the dais facing a dozen circular tables where ladies (and a handful of men) of a certain age are finishing up breakfast. I don't know if the speeches are to come or are done with. Either way I think I'll be more comfortable waiting in the hallway. I settle into a nearby easy chair and pick up a copy of 'Palo Alto This Week'. From what I can see this week in Palo Alto is much like every other week. Five minutes later the room starts to empty with much gibbering and nattering as the ladies head down the corridor. I get to my feet and intercept Isobel as she emerges alone.

"Miss Graham," I say, stepping in front of her.

"Mr. Bernardi," she replies. "You're getting to be something of a pest."

"I work at it," I say.

"I'm sure, but I have no time for you just now."

"Too bad," I say, tagging along as she starts for the lobby up ahead. "I need to speak to you about the alimony."

She stops and turns to face me.

"I beg your pardon."

"The alimony," I say again. "You know, the cash payments that Constance has delivered to her ex-husband every month. You do know about the alimony, don't you, if that's what it really is."

"I have no idea what you're talking about," she croaks, looking away, blinking her eyes and otherwise giving a good imitation of Pinocchio. Her nose is the only thing that doesn't give her away.

"Roy Perry told me the divorce was quick and final with no strings attached," I say. "Funny, I see strings and threads hanging all over the place, but if you won't give me a straight answer, maybe the police will have better luck."

"And what have the police to do with this?" she asks.

I move in close to her, as close as I can, violating her space just short of carnal knowledge.

"You seem to have forgotten that Amanda Broome has been killed and your bed pal Constance is coming into millions of dollars, even as Amanda's murder remains unsolved. Sorry to put it so crudely but I'm getting tired of playing footsies with you two women and if it takes the police to ask questions that demand answers, so be it. That's up to you."

Her skin color has gone from light peach to alabaster and her eyes betray a fear that surprises even me. What the hell have I stumbled onto? Suddenly her eyes glaze over and I think she's about to fall. I grab her.

"Must sit," she says quietly. I lead her to the easy chair I have just vacated and watch as she takes a small vial from her purse and extracts a tiny white pill which she pops under her tongue.

"Can I get you something?" I ask.

"No. I'll be all right," she whispers.

"Nitro?"

She nods.

"Isobel!"

I know before turning who it is. Constance Perry is approaching impatiently, her eyes beady with anger.

"Is this man bothering you?" she asks. "I suggest we call for hotel security."

Isobel shakes her head.

"No, that won't be necessary, Constance."

"I think it is," she replies.

"I said no!" Isobel says sharply. "And stop telling me how to live my life. I'm fed up with it."

Constance looks coldly at Isobel, apparently unused to rebellion from her paramour.

I smile engagingly.

"I was just asking your attorney for some information about your alimony payments to your ex-husband, Mrs. Perry. Oddly she says she knows nothing about them."

Constance looks sharply at Isobel who looks away, then shifts her attention back to me.

"Perhaps she does, Mr. Bernardi. You have heard of attorney-client privilege, I presume."

"Sure. I used to watch Perry Mason faithfully every week. I also know a little about blackmail, my favorite felony, second only to first degree murder."

"Blackmail? What on earth are you talking about?"

"Ten to twenty in most states, Mrs. Perry, unless you have a good lawyer. You do have a good lawyer, don't you, ma'am? One you can count on?" I look from one to the other, then smile and bid them a good day. This cage has been properly rattled. I can hear the rivets coming loose and I'm pretty sure the loudest rattle is coming from Isobel Graham. Constance Perry is cold, calculating and unflappable. Isobel reminds me of an bunny rabbit looking for a place to hide in a forest full of wolves.

Outside the hotel, Mick and I compare notes. I'm determined to get to Roy Perry as soon as possible, hoping I can reach him before he talks to Constance and they cook up some absurd explanation of Frederick's monthly cash deliveries. Meanwhile, Mick wants to check in with the police to find out if there have been any Frederick sightings. He'll show his credentials and claim Frederick skipped on bail a couple of years ago, stiffing Mick for five thousand dollars. We agree to touch base at the Burgundy Inn around five o'clock. I tell him about my meeting last evening with the prudish hotel manager, Leo Brickell. When he hears I've passed him off as an FBI agent he starts to laugh and is still laughing as he jogs across the street to his car.

I should have called ahead. Should have but didn't so when I find Roy Perry's office door locked and ask one of the other teachers on the floor if they know where I can find him, the guy just grins and says "Try the sixth hole." Seems Perry arranged his schedule to make sure he had Wednesdays off. Doctors' day for golf and Perry has become a regular part of the group.

By the time I get to the country club, it's almost one o'clock and I learn from the starter that Perry's group is probably just finishing up the third hole. He won't be off the course until three-thirty at the earliest, more like four. By now I'm hungry but I can't eat here. Members only. I head back to my car with the intention of returning by four o'clock. The good news is, if I can't reach the professor right away, neither can Constance. As I approach the parking lot I spot Hank Perry leaning against a little red sports car, chatting with a nubile young lady in the skimpiest of tennis outfits. She's a real knockout and Hank is all over her like maple syrup on a waffle. She doesn't seem to mind. A quick kiss as she pats him on the tush, then leaves as Hank watches her wiggle away.

"Nice," I say as I near him.

He looks at me and smiles.

"Nicer than nice, Mr. Bernardi. Nice and willing."

"Lucky you."

"All that and rich, too," Hank says. "Gloria Weidemeyer. Her old man runs an investment business. Offices in San Fran, San Jose and Santa Cruz. But she only has eyes for me."

I point to the sports car.

"What's this? New car?" I ask.

His face turns sour.

"A loaner and a real piece of crap. MG Midget. No leg room, no power, no nothin'."

"What happened to the 'B'"?

"Saturday morning, this asshole comes through a stop sign and slams my rear end. My guy tows it to his shop but he can't order parts till Monday. Worse he hasn't even got a loaner for me. Monday one of his guys delivers this piece of junk to my front door thinking I'd be happy. I wasn't and I'm not because I'm going to be driving this tin crate until next Tuesday at the earliest."

"Can't be all bad," I say. "You've still got room for your golf clubs."

"Barely," he smiles. "You looking for my Dad? I think he's out on the course."

"So I hear. I'll be back."

"Oh, say, I meant to ask you, Mr. Bernardi, what's with Amanda? I mean, I haven't heard anything about a funeral or a memorial, anything like that."

"The police still have her body," I say. "When they release it I expect her aunt will make arrangements."

"What?" he says bitterly. "A plastic bag and a hole in the ground?" Then: "Sorry. That was uncalled for."

"You don't care for the woman much, do you, Hank?"

He shrugs.

"Since she's always treated my Dad like crap and still does, no, I guess I don't."

"On the other hand," I say, "there's always the alimony."

"Alimony? What alimony? There's no alimony."

"Maybe I heard it wrong," I say with a shrug.

"I think maybe so," Hank says, swinging open the car door and scrunching himself behind the wheel. "Damned car was designed for six year olds," he grouses as he starts the engine. "See ya!" he waves as he pulls away and heads for the exit.

I find a Howard Johnson a few blocks away and order the fried clams, a favorite. No beer available so I settle for a Nehi and a side of cole slaw. I try to think of a meaningful way to fill the next couple of hours but can't and the minute hand on my watch creeps very slowly toward four o'clock. By the time I get back to the country club, Perry is off the course and I am told that he is in the men's smoker playing gin rummy with the other members of his foursome.

"It's the usual with those fellas, sir," says a geriatric porter. "A round of golf and an hour or two of beer and gin rummy at a penny point. Wednesdays and Saturdays like clockwork."

"Maybe if I just stuck my head in," I say.

"Couldn't let you do that, sir. The smoker's off limits to guests. Members only but if you like I can deliver a message."

I hand him a fin and tell him I like. He returns a couple of minutes later. The Professor can't be interrupted now but will be in his office at nine tomorrow morning. This is bad news. He may hear from Constance in the interim so I have no idea what to expect when we meet. I know this. I will be there at nine sharp which means I will spend another night at the Burgundy Inn. This commute between Bodega and Palo Alto has ceased to be amusing.

I've already called ahead to the front desk and booked a room for the night. Now I pull in to the parking lot, and go inside to find Mick is already seated at a back booth in the coffee shop, nursing an orange juice. As I sit Angela comes back into my life and I order a lemonade. Glumly, I tell Mick about my wasted afternoon. He smiles. It seems he has had better luck.

"Frederick?" I ask, hope in my heart.

"They caught up with him in Cloverdale, heading north in a stolen car, maybe heading for the border. Kid in a gas station recognized him from the news broadcasts, stalled him for ten minutes while the nearby Highway Patrol station swung into action. They're holding him until the local police can send a car to pick him up. Feel better?"

"Much," I say.

"So now all you have to worry about is the anonymous creep who came after you in the Oldsmobile."

"I know, I know," I say peevishly, "but that's not going to happen again."

"No, next time it'll be something else you're ill-equipped to deal with."

"Hey, I'm still in one piece."

"For now," Mick concedes. "You still need a keeper."

"What do you mean, still?" I ask. "What's going on, Mick?"

At that moment, Angela approaches the table.

"Excuse me, Mr. Bernardi, there's a call for you. A Miss Graham. You can take it on the white phone over there on the wall."

I share a quick look with Mick. All that cage rattling may have gotten us a break. I thank Angela and stride across the room to the phone.

"Mr. Bernardi, Isobel Graham."

"Yes, ma'am."

"I wasn't sure I'd find you there. I took a chance."

"Here and at your service, Ms. Graham."

"We need to talk."

"All right."

"I'm tied up the rest of the day. First thing tomorrow morning. My office. Nine o'clock."

I think about tomorrow morning and my nine o'clock at Roy Perry's office.

"Nine's not good, Ms. Graham. How about ten or ten-thirty?" Dead silence from her end. "Isobel, are you all right?"

"Yes. I mean, no. All right, ten o'clock then."

"You sound frightened. What is it?"

"Just nerves. There's something I have to tell you. I've been carrying it around far too long, Mr. Bernardi, and I have to tell someone besides the police."

"If you're in some kind of danger—"

"Tomorrow morning. Ten o'clock," she says and hangs up.

I return to the booth and repeat verbatim my conversation with Isobel Graham. Mick nods his head approvingly.

"Sounds promising," he says, "though I doubt it has any direct bearing on the death of Amanda Broome. It's that 'far too long' that doesn't fit."

"But it's progress, Mick."

"Oh, yes, it is that." He hesitates, "Look, Joe, I hate to bug out on you but I called home and Lydia told me that little Joe busted his ankle falling off his bicycle. I don't think it's too serious but they're keeping him overnight at the hospital and Lyd's a basket case so—"

"Go!" I say.

"I don't like leaving you like this so I'm going to send Kim—"

"I don't need Kim."

"You do."

"I don't. I'm going to see Graham and Perry in the morning and then scoot back to Bodega. I have my awe-inspiring pistol in my pocket and I'll be just fine. Now go home and see to your family."

He hesitates, then gets to his feet.

"I'll call you from the house for an update. No bullshit, amigo. I want it straight and if you need Kim, you've got her."

"Understood," I say. I stand and we embrace, then he turns and hurries from the coffee shop. I watch as he gets in his car and drives off. I'm not afraid but I do feel very alone and I don't like it. Not a bit.

I grab a sandwich and then retreat to my room. The television is lousy and the only thing I have to read is a Gideon bible. Finally I give up and slide under the covers after setting the alarm for 7:30. I needn't have bothered. Through a haze I hear knocking in the distance, come more awake and realize someone is rapping on my hotel room door. The clock on the nightstand reads 7:03. I stumble out of bed and answer the knock in my tee shirt and skivvies. Standing in the doorway is Chief Bridger.

"I thought I might find you here," he says. "Mind if I come in?" He doesn't wait for a reply but pushes past me and gives my humble quarters the once over. He turns to me. "What time did you come back here last night?"

"I didn't. I never left."

"Can anybody verify that?"

"I don't know. What's this about?"

"Do you know a woman named Isobel Graham?"

"Yes. I have a meeting scheduled with her at ten o'clock at her office."

"Not any more you don't," Bridger says. "She's in the hospital. Nitroglycerin overdose. Possible suicide attempt. Maybe something worse. Medical examiner can't say. We found your card on her desk at home and your name penciled in on her appointment calendar at her office."

"How is she?"

"She's still unconscious but she'll live. What was your meeting about?"

"Confidential."

Bridger arches an eyebrow. "Really? In that case you'd better have a witness who was sitting in that chair all night and will swear that you never left the room. Anything short of that and you're coming down to headquarters where I will question you less politely."

"The subject of our meeting was to be a woman of great reputation in this city, a woman of whom one must never breathe a negative word."

"Constance Perry."

"Yes."

"Why didn't you say so?"

"You told me not to."

"You know, you're not as funny as you think you are."

"So I've been told."

"Is your car with the valet?"

"I self-parked."

"Too bad. According to the neighbor across the street Miss Graham had a visitor between seven-thirty and ten."

"Male? Female?"

"She never got a look. The visitor was driving a large four door car, some sort of dark color, possibly green, make unknown. The woman knows nothing about automobiles but says the car was gone a few minutes after ten. At ten thirty she took her dog for a walk, noticed a broken sprinkler head on Miss Graham's property spewing water every place but the lawn. Miss Graham's lights were still on so the neighbor went over and rang the doorbell. Getting no response, she peered in the front living room window and saw Miss Graham lying motionless on the floor. She called an ambulance. The doctor who treated Miss Graham said another thirty minutes and she would have been dead."

"For the record, Chief, my car is a cream colored Bentley."

"Easily verified," he says.

"You say the visitor drove a large car, possibly green?"

"Possibly but the neighbor can't swear to it."

Odd. I keep seeing Constance Perry's green Lincoln town car but of course, that isn't possible. Frederick's in the pokey and the woman doesn't drive. Or does she?

# CHAPTER FIFTEEN

Bridger doesn't throw the cuffs on me and haul me down to the station. In fact we part amiably and I believe I have persuaded him that I am a straight shooter. I had asked him about visiting the hospital once Isobel Graham was awake. He said he'd give it some thought but that was as far as he would commit. The good news is, it's still early enough for me to keep my nine o'clock with Roy Perry even if it means forgoing my usual breakfast in favor of a hardboiled egg and a container of coffee.

I am only four minutes late but Perry is compelled to chide me about my tardiness. When I tell him about Isobel's hospitalization and my lengthy chat with the chief of police, he apologizes.

"She's not the type," he says.

"What type is that?" I ask.

"Suicide."

"You know her well?"

"Only casually but well enough to know there's no quit in her. Whatever Isobel's problems, she wouldn't try to solve them with an overdose of pills."

"Maybe a lover's quarrel?"

"Certainly not that," Perry snorts, "although I'm the last one to ask about the subtleties of a lesbian relationship, especially where my ex-wife is concerned."

"Constance may have visited her at her home last evening though I can't figure out how since she can't drive."

"What do you mean, 'can't drive'? Of course she can drive. She chooses not to, that's all."

"You're sure about that?"

"Of course I am. When we were first married she drove all the time. Then one day a kid pulling a wagon jumped out in front of her. The kid was hurt but survived. The dog being towed in the wagon was killed and after that Constance let her license lapse and left the driving to me. But know how? Absolutely." He regards me curiously. "But you didn't come here to talk about Isobel's demise. What's on your mind, Mr. Bernardi?"

"Same old, same old," I say. "Who killed Amanda Broome and tried to pin it on Rod Taylor?"

"Isobel?" he asks skeptically.

"Doubtful. I'd like to talk about the alimony."

"What alimony?"

I can't help but laugh. Thousands of dollars changing hands every month and when I ask about it, everybody gives me the same blank stare.

"Two thousand dollars a month, most recently delivered to you by hand by your ex-wife's chauffeur."

"I don't know what you're talking about," Perry says indignantly.

"Of course you don't. Now here's my question. Did these payments begin immediately after your divorce? No, I doubt that. Constance didn't have that kind of money then. But after her brother was killed and she became the executrix of the estate and the guardian of his daughter, that all changed."

"You're uttering nonsense, Mr. Bernardi," Perry says angrily.

"Am I? Did you know they have Frederick Shurling in custody facing a raft of charges. How long before he starts looking for a deal in exchange for what he knows."

"He knows nothing."

"What have you got on her, Professor, that's worth two thousand dollars a month, month in and month out?"

"I think you'd better leave."

"Two thousand a month, that pays a lot of bills, and you sure don't have to risk your own money in the stock market to get it. By the way, you never did tell me the name of your broker in San Jose."

"Leave now, Mr. Bernardi, or I will call campus security."

I get to my feet.

"No need, Professor. You've told me all I really need to know. I'm beginning to get the picture and it's looking ugly, sir. Very ugly."

With that I turn on my heel and walk out. On the way to my car my head is spinning with a dozen different thoughts and I'm unhappy with all of them. Someone once said, 'Truth will out." I don't know what planet he was living on but it must have been populated with mindless optimists. I very much fear that the two thousand dollar a month secret is doomed to be locked in secrecy for eternity. Constance Perry is a hard-nose. So is her ex-husband. Frederick Shurling might be softened up if he was offered the right kind of deal but there's always the possibility he didn't actually know what the money was for. That leaves only Isobel Graham who might have tried to check out last night. Either that or someone tried to help her out the door. I guess the only way I'm going to find out is to ask her. I start up the Bentley and limp my way toward the main road.

I'm a couple of blocks away from the hospital when I am hit by the sudden realization that I may be the only outsider who knows what's been going on. In a fit of self-preservation I pull over next to a phone booth and place a call to Sergeant Hayes in Santa Rosa. I'd thought momentarily about sharing what I know with Chief Bridger here in Palo Alto and discarded it immediately. He seems too blinded by Constance Perry's status to listen objectively. Hayes I trust. Bridger I don't and for my own safety, someone else besides me has got to know what I think I know.

When Hayes comes on the line, I share it all. The monthly payments, the denials by everyone involved, the troubled call from Isobel saying she needed to tell me something, something she could no longer carry around with her after all these years and finally the mysterious overdose that would have killed her had it not been for a broken sprinkler head and a concerned neighbor.

"What are you saying, Joe?" Hayes asks.

"You know what I'm saying. You're the cop. Add it up."

"Blackmail."

"Most likely."

"You have no proof," Hayes says.

"You like the fairy tale about the alimony better?"

Silence. Then he says, "What's this got to do with the murder of Amanda Broome?"

"I don't know. Something. I know this, Sarge. Constance was about to lose her meal ticket when Amanda inherited and now she'll be able to buy and sell God."

"Joe, the woman was in Palo Alto when Amanda was killed and she has a dozen witnesses to prove it."

"Gee. Only a dozen? And where was Frederick Shurling?"

"Joe, you've been in the movie business too long. Charlie Chan is not real life. What do you think? You think she killed Amanda? Maybe you think she also killed her brother thirteen years ago?"

"You said it, Sarge, not me."

"Oh, please—"

"She came home to the house with her lesbian lover, claimed to have found her brother dead on the floor, shot twice. A wooden mallet and a chisel were found beside the body. The wall safe had gouge marks on the hinges but it hadn't been opened. A classic setup.

We're supposed to believe that Broome arrived home, surprised a burglar and got shot for his trouble. A short time later Constance and Isobel show up, find him and call the police. The house sits on a large plot of ground, isolated from neighbors who didn't see anyone come or go and also did not hear the gunshots. The ladies tell their story and who's to say if it's true or not?"

"Thin. Very thin," he says.

"Look, I'm not asking you to do anything about it, I just want you to be aware of it in case something happens to me like a car accident or a refrigerator falls on me."

"Like I said, you've been watching too many B movies."

"We'll see," I riposte cleverly.

As soon as I arrive at the hospital I get the good news. Isobel Graham has recently awakened and is apparently out of danger. The bad news is, she's being kept isolated pending an official statement to the police which she has yet to give. Her medical team is still being cautious about her condition. I know this because I run into Chief Bridger on the ground floor lobby of the hospital. When I ask if I can speak to her, he suggests I check with him later in the day. I believe this is code for 'This is police business and who the hell are you to be sticking your nose in where it doesn't belong?'. I could be wrong, of course, but I don't think so. I thank him gratefully and leave but I don't go far. I slide behind the wheel of my car where I have a good view of the front entrance. Ten minutes later, Bridger emerges with an aide and a uniformed cop and drive off. I slip off my jacket and lay it on the backseat, then return to the lobby, find the nearest phone booth and call the hospital. My name is Joseph Bernardi, I say. I am Miss Graham's law partner. I just heard the terrible news. What room is she in? 445? Thank you. What do you mean, no visitors? What do you mean, 'suicide watch'? This is absurd. I will speak to the police about this and, yes, I will see my partner even if it means having to get a court order, you can count on it. I abruptly hang up.

I wander around trying to look as official as possible, tracking down the operating rooms. Once there I rummage around and find the waste bin that holds used scrubs and grab a set along with a cap and a respiratory mask. I put them on (a lousy fit but they'll do) and head for the elevators. When I emerge on the fourth floor I find it bustling with activity. Good. What's one more doctor, more or less? I peer into a couple of rooms. In the second one, the lights are out and the patient, an elderly woman, is fast asleep. I grab the clipboard at the foot of her bed and start down the corridor. A couple of nurses wish me a good morning. I give them a curt nod. All the hospital doctors I've ever met are good at curt nods. It saves them from actually having to talk to anyone.

It doesn't take me long to find Room 445. There's a folding chair next to the door but it's unoccupied. Then I see him. A good looking young uniformed officer with brown wavy hair is chatting with an equally good looking candy striper at the nurses station. He smiles, she giggles and then, when his back is turned, I open the door to 445 and slip inside. The blinds are partially drawn, the lights are out, the room is dim.

Isobel is lying in bed, eyes half open, the head of the bed slightly elevated. I cross over and look down at her.

"Miss Graham," I say, tugging down my mask. "It's me. Joe Bernardi."

"I know you," she says quietly.

"We were supposed to meet this morning at your office."

"Were we?"

"Yes, you'd called me. You were troubled about something. You needed to speak to me."

"Did I? I don't remember."

"What happened last night at your house? You had company."

"Yes, Constance came for dinner. It was a big surprise. I hadn't invited her. Naturally, I was pleased."

She's staring off into space, disconnected, as if talking to herself.

"Naturally," I say. "What did you talk about?"

"Nothing. Everything. It was quite enjoyable. Great fun."

"Did you talk about the night her brother died?"

"Oh, no. We never talk about that. Never."

"How about the alimony?"

"That either," she says, still unfocused. "He's a terrible man, you know. Mean and vindictive and selfish."

"Roy, you mean."

"Yes, Roy. Her ex-husband. Evil. A very evil man."

"He demanded alimony," I suggest.

"Constance said that's what we should call it."

"But it wasn't really alimony, was it?"

"Of course not," she replies irritably.

"Was he alive when you arrived at the house? Andrew, I mean. Her brother." She doesn't answer but continues to stare at some inconsequential spot on the far wall. "Isobel?"

"I told you, we never talk about that," she replies.

"Why did Constance shoot him, Isobel?" More silence. "She must have had a reason."

"We mustn't talk about it. Constance is always telling me that. Our secret. The secret that binds our love. She's so bossy about it."

"But you did talk about it, didn't you? Last night, when Constance came to dinner."

" She wanted to talk about it. She was afraid I was going to tell others. I said I didn't want to talk about Andrew or that night. I wanted us to be gay and funny the way we had been for all these many years. And then I had my attack."

"Another attack? Your heart?"

"Yes. I took a pill."

"One pill?"

"Yes, of course."

"Maybe you took several by mistake," I say.

She shakes her head.

"One pill, always one pill. Constance helped me to a chair and brought me some wine."

"And then what happened?"

"I was tired. I don't remember."

"Did she help you into bed?"

"I don't remember."

Suddenly the door flies open and the room is flooded with light from the corridor. I turn. Bridger is framed in the doorway momentarily and then strides in angrily followed by a uniformed officer.

"What the hell do you think you're doing?" he demands to know.

"Obtaining information you'll want to know about."

"The hell you say, Bernardi," he growls. "I no sooner get back to my office when I get this call from the hospital about some law partner demanding to see Miss Graham and I know Goddamn well she hasn't got a law partner. Then when your name is mentioned, I am sure you are up to no good. Sergeant, arrest this man and take him to headquarters."

"Yes, sir," the uniform says grabbing my arm.

"Arrest? What for?"

"Interfering with a police investigation. Get him out of my sight."

"Yes, sir," and with that the sergeant drags me out of the room. In the corridor gawkers stare as a doctor in green scrubs is hauled away to the pokey. One to tell the grandchildren.

# CHAPTER SIXTEEN

It didn't take them long to book me and even less time to toss me in the lock up at the rear of the first floor. Not a cell, really, more like a cage and there are three of them. The other two are empty. I had expected them to take me to the city jail but when I heard one of the officers mumble something to a cohort about the chief tearing this wise guy a new one, I surmised that I was the wise guy. I was proven correct a short time later when I was led from the cage to Bridger's office.

The atmosphere is not quite as festive as it was the last time I was here. I am plunked unceremoniously into a chair as Bridger stares at me. I wait for him to say something and when he doesn't I decide to kick off the conversation.

"Did you question her?" I ask. "You really should, you know?"

"Did I ask you to speak?" Bridger says.

"No, sir."

"Then don't. I don't get you, Bernardi. You're a meddlesome, quarrelsome buttinski who has trouble comprehending the English language. Do you come by this talent naturally or are you self taught?"

"Got it from my father. He worked for the FBI after he proved he was too smart to work as a city cop."

Bridger smiles. "See what I mean? There you go. Just can't keep that mouth of yours shut."

Smug bastard. At the risk of being belted around by a rubber hose, I decide to give it to him straight.

"No, I can't, Chief, not when I'm being bullied by a cop who cares more about politics than he does about criminal justice, who kowtows to the city's poobahs to make sure he gets invited to the right parties and who thinks that his tin badge gives him the powers of the Mikado. Now let me make my phone call to my lawyer and then put me back in my cage. I am in no mood to be lectured to by the likes of you."

Bridger leans back in his chair and stares at me with some amusement. "Well, I would like to accommodate you, Mr. Bernardi, I really would, but I don't have the time, the patience or the energy to deal with Ezra Crabtree so I am going to let you go. But in the meantime, just for my own amusement, why don't you tell me what I should be questioning Miss Graham about?"

"You won't like it."

"Suppose you let me decide that."

Okay, Chief, if you want Constance Perry pulled down off her pedestal, I will be glad to oblige. I tell him in detail about my talk with Isobel, everything she said, as well as what I surmise. His face is a mask but he is listening intently. When I finish he sits quietly for a few moments, thoughtfully tenting his hands in front of his face.

"Thirteen years ago. I wasn't Chief then."

"I didn't think you were."

"Matter of fact, I didn't even live in Palo Alto. Came here a couple of years later, in case you were assuming that I am some dumb hick cop who can't tell a real burglary from a staged crime scene."

"Never said you were stupid, Chief, just overly self-assured."

"Murder's a pretty serious allegation, Mr. Bernardi. Did Miss Graham actually say she saw Miz Perry shoot her brother?"

"Not specifically, no. She was just getting to it when you walked in the door."

He nods.

"Well, I listened very carefully to what you had to say and specifically, it wasn't much. A lot of non-answers, hinting around and guesswork."

"And I am not a trained policeman, wise in the ways of interrogation. I promise you this. The woman has a tale to tell and she wants to tell it but she's scared to death. Whether that's fear of prison or of Constance Perry, I do not know."

"Well, thank you for your input, Mr. Bernardi, and now you may leave. And I mean leave my headquarters and my town and do not come back. Do I make myself clear?"

"You do."

"Find your way out."

"And a pleasant good day to you as well, Chief," I say, rising from my chair and heading for the door. I turn."I don't suppose I could get a lift back to the hospital to pick up my car." Bridger just smiles. "That's what I thought," I say.

I leave the building and step out into the sunlight. It is a beautiful cloudless day. The temperature is moderate. A great day, in fact, if I hadn't just been unceremoniously exiled from this charming and mostly friendly little city. My work isn't done here and it looks as if it won't be. I've done what I can for Rod. Now it's going to be up to Hayes and Henrietta Boyle to discover the truth about Amanda's death. As to what happened at the Broome house thirteen years ago, I guess the truth will remain buried forever. Isobel Graham wants it to come out but deep down she's too afraid and if she does speak up, what proof is there except for her word? Constance Perry escaped detection once and I am convinced she is doing it again and there is nothing I can do about it.

My thoughts turn to an immediate problem. I need to find a

cab to take me back to the hospital. Then, as I walk down to the sidewalk, a cruiser pulls into the parking lot and stops near the front entrance. Two cops get out and open the rear door. I can see that the back seat is a cage for transporting prisoners and the star of the moment is Frederick Shurling who has been brought back from Cloverdale to face justice at the hands of Alonzo Bridger. I stop in mid-stride and turn to look back at the building as Frederick is hustled through the front door. A thought permeates my over-worked grey matter. I'm not quite through with Palo Alto and Palo Alto is not quite through with me.

I rap loudly on Bridger's office door and then walk in. He looks up and glowers.

"We said goodbye, Mr. Bernardi."

"Your boys just brought in Frederick Shurling."

"My boys are good at their jobs."

"I want to press charges."

"For what?"

"Assault with a deadly weapon. Schurling tried to kill me in the parking lot of The Pig Sty."

"We have only your word on that."

"I have a witness. A college kid. I can have him in here tomorrow, maybe even later today. Depends on how quick I can find him."

"And what's all this about a deadly weapon?"

"Back in Germany, Schurling was a professional boxer which means he's looking at ten to twenty minimum."

"We've already got him in for assaulting an officer and stealing his weapon."

"A really good lawyer might get that knocked down to a misdemeanor. If so, Schurling walks. I want to give you some leverage, Chief. Talk to Isobel Graham, listen to her story. If you put the squeeze on Schurling, he'll back her up."

"And why would he do that?"

"Because I'd have the assault charges dropped. No complaining witness, no case."

Bridger shakes his head.

"You're really convinced that Constance Perry killed her brother."

"I am and you will be, too, if you bother to look into it."

Bridger stares at me thoughtfully.

"You've got big balls, brother, coming back in here like this."

"I don't know what's good for me," I say. "Never have."

"All right, I'll amend the complaint and I'll question Isobel Graham."

"That's all I ask, Chief. Thanks."

"Now leave."

"Going," I assure him and I duck out of there in search of a taxi.

It's pushing four when I get back to the Burgundy Inn after stopping at the hospital to pick up my car. Once in my room, I place a call to the production manager, Norman Deming, in Bodega.

"What's happening?" I ask when he comes on the line.

"We're gonna have to shoot on Saturday, travel on Sunday and that's if we're really lucky."

"How's Rod holding up?"

"What you'd expect. Having the fiance here helps but if we have to go back to L.A. without him we're screwed. One of the studio lawyers is trying to work something out with the Boyle woman. A guarantee of appearance, some kind of legal dodge, I think. I doubt she's buying it."

"Reporters?"

"All over the place. The studio sent up a publicity guy. Schmidt, I think—"

"Eddie Schmidt. I know him. Good man."

"He's hired a security company and the shooting sites are tight as a drum. Meantime, he's wandering around town, schmoozing the media guys with booze and beer. It could be worse. How're you doing?"

"Not so good. The cops are anxious to kick me out of town. They may succeed."

"Can't win 'em all."

On those words of wisdom, he hangs up and I lean back on my pillow, staring at the ceiling. I need to think. I close my eyes. A couple of minutes later, the phone rings. I reach for it, noticing that the clock alarm next to the bed has gone haywire. It reads 6:08.

"Hello."

"Get over here. Now," comes a snarl.

"Chief?"

He doesn't answer but he doesn't have to. Groggily I get up, realizing that I am hungry. I never had lunch. I splash cold water on my face, shuffle outside to my car and make my way back to Bryant Street. I'm not feeling good about this. What fresh hell has he got in store for me now?

I rap tentatively on his door. No answer. I turn the handle and peer in. Empty.

"He's in the cafeteria," says a voice passing by which turns out to be a uniformed cop. Without looking back at me, he points to a corridor that juts out to the right.

Bridger is sitting at a small table in the corner of a small cafeteria which apparently services not only police headquarters but the fire department offices next door as well. I approach. He's having a bowl of white clam chowder with oyster crackers. He looks up.

"Mind if I join you?" I ask.

He points to the opposite chair.

"Help yourself but if you're hungry get yourself a tray."

"I think I'll do that."

"Soup's good. So are the burgers. Stay away from the chili."

"Right."

It takes me ten minutes to get a cheeseburger and a Dr. Pepper. When I return to the table, he's finished eating and is consulting a small spiral bound notebook. I don't interrupt. Finally he looks over at me.

"I questioned Isobel Graham," he says.

"Did she admit what happened?"

"She denied everything," Bridger says. "And she was lying. It was so obvious you wonder how she ever got to be a lawyer." He hesitates. "Whether you believe it or not, Mr. Bernardi, and I really don't care if you do or you don't, but I am a pretty good cop. That being said, I missed this one. The lady was too important in the community and you were too big a pain in the ass. I won't make that mistake again."

"She'll crack," I say.

"I'm not so sure. When she learned what had happened, the overdose, the wine, I think she figured Constance Perry tried to kill her."

"All the more reason to get it out in the open."

"Logically, yes, but she knows she's an accessory even if she only helped stage the scene. Prison for a woman her age won't be a lot of fun."

"What's Frederick say?"

"He wants a lawyer."

"Good," I say. "A lawyer might talk some sense into him. He wasn't around thirteen years ago and the old girlfriend alibis him for the time I was being run off the road in the hills above Bodega so aside from the weapons beef and our scuffle in the parking lot, all he's really guilty of is delivering cash and flexing his muscles in public."

Bridger actually laughs though he tries to stifle it.

"I'll work on him again. The woman, too. How's the cheese-burger?"

"Good."

He nods. "Stick around town tomorrow. I might need you," he says as he stands. "Back to work. Finish your burger." He walks away.

I had planned to drive back to Bodega Bay first thing in the morning. Now that I have suddenly become Bridger's bosom ally, I decide to stay. I may be needed to apply heat to Isobel or Frederick or both. Come Friday morning and it's breakfast in the coffee shop where I buy a copy of the Palo Alto Weekly newspaper. It has a four page spread covering the filming in Bodega Bay with dozens of photos by ace photographer, Gracie James. The by-line for the text goes to Joseph Gillis. I have to laugh. Joe Gillis is the down at the heels writer played by Bill Holden in 'Sunset Boulevard'. I see the fine hand of Universal's press department deeply involved in this spread.

With no place to go and nothing to do but wait in case Bridger needs me I return to my room. I toss the weekly newspaper on the coffee table and flop on the bed to call Bunny at the office. She is cheery but busy. All is well at home. The turtle has survived his toothache and after school, Yvette is hard at work writing a very long and very exciting story about an old man on a park bench and a talking snail. Jill would be so proud. I tell her it looks like I'll be home Sunday, Monday at the latest. Not much is new but I haven't quit. Not yet. I blow kisses and hang up. Three seconds later the phone rings. It's Bridger. I'm needed.

I get into my wounded car which is getting harder and harder to drive each time I get behind the wheel. I look both ways carefully before pulling out onto the street. I look across to the opposite sidewalk where yet another meter maid is making her way from vehicle to vehicle looking for miscreants who have overstayed their welcome. The town seems to be crawling with these babes. Maybe it's true. Maybe these nickels and dimes are how Palo Alto funds its annual budget. I've learned that in the state of California, anything is possible, even if it makes no sense at all.

I'm looking through a plate glass window into an interrogation room. Frederick is cuffed to the table. Sitting next to him is a hawk-nosed bald man with a yellow lined legal pad in front of him. This, I surmise, is Frederick's lawyer. At the end of the table is a burly guy in shirt sleeves wearing a shoulder holster. He has wisely not brought his weapon into the room. This is one of the two interrogators. I think he is supposed to be the 'good cop'. The other guy was definitely the 'bad cop'. To be honest, it's hard to tell the difference. Anyway, I see them but they don't see me because their side of the glass is a mirror. Standing beside me is Chief Bridger. He's fidgeting and I can tell he's seen enough.

"Time for the first team to take over," he says. "Follow me."

We exit into the corridor and step into the room next door. Bridger claps the cop on his shoulder.

"Good work, Duffy. I'll take it from here."

"Right, Chief."

Duffy leaves and Bridger points me to a nearby empty chair. I sit and find myself staring at Frederick who is coldly staring back. We make a game of it for a few seconds until Frederick's lawyer elbows him and the burly ex-boxer turns his attention to Chief Bridger.

"We're trying to help you out here, Mr. Schurling," the Chief says. "Apparently you're not interested."

"I didn't do nothing," Frederick says.

Bridger smiles. "For a man who didn't do nothing, you're going to spend an awful lot of time in prison, my friend. I figure when you get out, you'll be at least fifty, maybe older. Resisting arrest, assaulting a police officer, theft of a firearm, not to mention your vicious attack on Mr. Bernardi here. Maybe your attorney has convinced you that you didn't do nothing. I think a jury will see otherwise."

I look over at the big beaked baldy and see that he is staring at me intently.

"You are the aggrieved party?" he asks me.

"I am."

"The police claim you might be willing to withdraw your complaint?"

"Under certain circumstances. Yes."

The lawyer looks at Bridger.

"And the other charges?"

"We could be persuaded to knock them down to misdemeanors but this offer expires when we leave this room which, I must warn you, could be minutes from now."

The lawyer leans over and whispers in Frederick's ear. Frederick whispers back. Whisper, whisper, whisper. Finally Frederick looks over at Bridger. "What you want to know?" he asks.

"Each month you have been delivering cash to Mr. Roy Perry at his home in Los Altos Hills, is that right?"

"Yes."

"What was the money for?"

"I don't know."

"What were you told it was for?"

"The lady says alimony. Is a lie. Is for something else."

"What something else?"

"I don't know."

"Did you get a receipt?"

"No."

"Why not?"

"The lady didn't want one. The man, I don't think he would have given me one even if I ask."

"I'll try again. What do you think the money was for. Come, come, Mr. Schurling. You were there three years. You must have figured out something."

Frederick looks over at his lawyer who nods slightly.

"One day I hear them talking. Mrs. Constance and the other lady, her girlfriend. They are fighting. Something about the night the brother died. The girlfriend is frightened. She thinks the teacher is going to say something. Mrs. Constance says he won't, that he can be dealt with to make sure he never talks to anybody, ever. The other lady says no, she won't be part of anything like that. Not again."

"Those were her words? Not again?"

"That is what she says."

The voices drone on. It's coming out now. The whole sordid story. It's not proof, it's hearsay, but it gives Bridger a peek into what really happened and leverage to use against Isobel Graham. The questions keep coming, so do the answers. Frederick has a little more to contribute, not a lot, but I am only half-listening because something is bothering me and I can't pin down what it is. Something I heard, something I saw. It's there just out of reach. I snap back to the present as I realize everyone is standing. Schurling is being released into the custody of his attorney who will make him available when needed and Bridger and I are headed for his office.

"Good work, Joe," he says. "Thanks to you we've stumbled onto something I never could have imagined."

"It's a long way to conviction," I say.

"We'll get there," he replies and then smiles. "And then think about all the money we've saved the city by not having to bring Schurling to trial. An added bonus."

And just then, as he's walking into his office, it comes to me.

# CHAPTER SEVENTEEN

"Parking tickets?"

"A parking ticket," I say. "Last Saturday afternoon in the Alta and Hope area where the blue and white Olds was stolen and then returned.."

"The car that chased you all over hell's half acre?" Bridger says.

"That's the one."

He flops down behind his desk.

"Well, I'm not going to make the mistake of ignoring you again, Joe, so tell me."

"A man or, perhaps more likely a woman, wants to get rid of me by shoving me and my car down into a ravine on the way to Bodega Bay. She— and for the moment, let's say she—she drives around looking for a car she can steal because she certainly doesn't want to use her own. Much too dangerous in case she's spotted or even worse, fails. So she finds this powerful Oldsmobile with the keys in the ignition. She's already parked nearby. She drives off, comes after me, I survive, and she drives the stolen car back to the city to return it to more or less the place where she found it. She has to. What's she going to do? Abandon it in the mountains and walk back to town?"

"Go on."

"There are no parking spots so she leaves it in the vacant lot and goes to get her own car but more than ninety minutes have elapsed and she finds a ticket on the windshield. She gets in the car and drives off, maybe throwing the ticket on the floor or in the glove compartment."

"So," Bridger says, "we find the meter maid's copy of the ticket and maybe we find the guy—excuse me, the gal—who tried to run you off the road."

"Precisely."

He thinks about it for a minute and then stands up, heading for the door.

"Follow me," he says.

I tag along down the hallway to another room. We go in and he scans the labels on the filing cabinets for a few moments, then pulls out a drawer and starts to riff through one of the file folders. He freezes, then slowly extracts one of the tickets from the folder, studies it and then hands it to me.

At 5:15 on Saturday afternoon a white Cadillac Coupe de Ville was cited for overtime parking in a metered parking space near the intersection of Alta and Hope. The vanity license plate on the car read 'R PERRY'.

I look up at Bridger.

"Why don't we pay a call on the Professor?" he says.

Twenty minutes later we drive up in the Chief's car to Roy Perry's house in Los Altos Hills. The Cadillac is parked in the driveway. There is no sign of a sports car, either the MGB or the little red Midget.

After two rings of the doorbell, Perry opens the door. He's wearing slacks, a windbreaker, and a Los Altos Hills CC golf cap, a departure from his usual tweedy look. On the foyer floor behind him is a suitcase.

"Good afternoon, Chief. Mr. Bernardi. I'd invite you in but I'm in something of a hurry."

"Going somewhere?" the Chief asks.

"San Francisco. My son is competing in the California Open golf tournament at the Olympic Club this weekend."

"This won't take long," Bridger says, walking past him into the house. I follow. I think Perry would like to object but he doesn't. He shuts the door and follows us into the living room where Bridger is looking around, admiring his surroundings.

"Nice house, Professor Perry," he says. "Nice house, nice neighborhood. I'm envious."

Perry throws a nervous look in my direction, remembering our last conversation.

"Look, if this is about the cash Constance has been giving me every month, I think there's been a big misunderstanding. I'm not a wealthy man and my son, Hank, has always been special to her so she generously has been helping out so Hank and I can live a life style that gives my boy the best chance for success in life. It's nothing formal, nothing in writing. Just old fashioned generosity."

Bridger nods.

"I don't believe I asked you anything about any money, Professor."

Again he looks at me.

"Well, I just assumed, I mean, I—"

"Last Saturday you got a parking ticket in Palo Alto."

"No."

"Oh, yes. Want to tell me about it?"

"I just said, you're mistaken."

"I don't think so. Someone stole a car from that area and followed Mr. Bernardi as he was returning to Bodega Bay. That someone tried to run him off the road in a stolen car, tried to kill him, and failing that, returned to Palo Alto. Does any of that sound familiar, Doctor?"

"I told you—"

"I know what you told me," Bridger says sharply. "I'm giving you a chance to rethink your answer. Were you in Palo Alto Saturday afternoon? Did you get a traffic ticket? Did you try to kill Mr. Bernardi?"

"Ridiculous. I would never try to harm anyone." He hesitates and a frown crosses his face. "Saturday afternoon, you say. I play golf on Saturdays, always, and then gin rummy and then—Now wait a minute. What time Saturday afternoon was this?"

"Say between three and six."

Perry shakes his head.

"I'm so stupid. Last Saturday we decided to skip the gin game. The other guys had things to do and I needed to do some shopping. It was so out of my routine that I forgot. As for the ticket, no, I didn't get one. When I finally got back to my car I saw on the meter that my time had expired and I remembered thinking I was very lucky that the meter maid had missed me. I guess maybe she did write the ticket and maybe some kids grabbed it and ripped it up or put it on someone else's car, as a joke, you know. But steal a car and try to commit murder? No, Chief, that's not me. No, it is not."

The questioning continues. What stores did he shop in? What did he buy? Not a lot. Much of it was window shopping. He picked up a couple of tools in a hardware store and some grooming items in a Rexall but they were crowded and he doubts if anyone will remember him. Finally Bridger has had enough and gets to his feet. He may have more questions. Stay available. Absolutely, Perry says. We head for the door and I can't stay quiet anymore, having waited in vain for Bridger to ask the question he never asked.

"By the way, Doc," I say, "what do you know about the death of Andrew Broome?"

He looks at me sharply.

"What?"

"Andrew Broome, your ex-wife's brother. Some years ago."

"I know nothing except what was in the papers and what Constance told me. He was killed by a burglar."

"And you don't know any different?"

"Of course not. What the hell are you talking about?"

"Joe."

Bridger grabs me by the elbow, squeezing tight. It's his way of saying, not now. A few minutes later, he and I are out front sitting in his car as Perry locks up, hauls his suitcase to the Caddy and then drives away.

"I wasn't ready to ask about that."

"Sorry. You're right. I'm a buttinsky."

"It isn't fatal," he says with a smile.

"So what do you think?" I ask.

"He's lying," Bridger says, the smile fading.

"How do you know?"

"I'm a highly trained detective, Joe. My instincts are keen and they never fail me. Besides I happen to know that the hardware store on that street closes at noon. I tried to buy a chain saw there two weeks ago." He smiles. It's the second time I've seen a human being behind that facade. Maybe he's decided that I'm not an asshole after all.

"Blackmail's an ugly crime, Joe," he says, "and the penalties are severe. My guess is he figured you were getting too close, that his cozy little deal might come to light, the payments would stop and worst case, he'd end up in prison."

"What next then?" I ask.

"I start to dig. This has been going on a long time. Chances are mistakes were made, there may be some sort of a trail, and Isobel Graham is a weak link. Come on, let's get back to town."

Back at headquarters I pick up my car and drive back to the Burgundy Inn. I'm no longer worried about Alonzo Bridger. I wasn't totally wrong about him but I wasn't totally right either. He's like a hound dog on the scent and I feel confident that Perry's head will be mounted on Bridger's office wall within a week. Two thousand dollars a month tax-free, that buys a lot of creature comforts and Roy Perry wasn't about to give them up to an obnoxious little creep like Amanda. Sad. I'd heard it said he was a pretty good teacher, liked and respected by his students but money can be, and often is, the great destroyer of otherwise honorable men.

I park in the lot and head inside, stopping at the coffee shop to ask that a club sandwich and a small carafe of coffee be delivered to my room. I have calls to make and no time to waste. I call Bunny at the newspaper office. She's at a luncheon honoring some local politician that's been in office for so long, William Howard Taft bounced him on his knee. These guys ought to know when to quit but they don't and my wife has to suffer through undercooked chicken and overcooked broccoli to prove it. Her assistant will tell her I called. I leave a number. Next I try Sergeant Hayes at the Sheriff's Office in Santa Clara. He's on another line. Same routine. I leave my number and hang up.

There's a knock on my door. I get it. A waiter has brought my sandwich and coffee which he places on the table. I sign the check and give him two bucks and sit down to eat, waiting for the phone to ring. I pick up the Palo Alto weekly and again scan the article about the filming in Bodega Bay. I admire Gracie's work. She knows what to do with a camera. This time around I spot a picture of me. It's small and down in the corner but I look pretty good. The caption describes me as Joseph Bernardi, best selling author. It gives me a mini-chill. Next to me is a shot of three crew members putting together the phony wharf at the Gaffney place. I recognize two of them, Harv and Kiwi, then squint looking at a third guy who looks vaguely familiar. He has a hammer in his hand and a grin on his face. At least I think it's a grin. The image is so small I can barely make him out.

The phone rings. I pick up.

"Honey?" I say hopefully.

"Sorry, Joe, I like you a lot but I'm spoken for." The voice belongs to Sergeant Hayes.

"Thought you were my wife," I say.

"Sorry to disappoint you. What's up?"

"I'm in Palo Alto and I think we're making progress down here."

"Tell me."

I fill him in on everything including Chief Bridger's belief, and mine, that Roy Perry is lying and that he most likely tried to kill me to keep me quiet.

"Uh,huh," Hayes says, "and what exactly has this to do with the murder of Amanda Broome?"

"Everything because she was killed before she could inherit many millions of dollars in about seven weeks."

"That sounds like a theory."

"It is but it makes a lot more sense than believing that a well-known and successful actor can't find a better way to deal with a blatantly stupid stalker than to slash her throat. And don't tell me you disagree because you're smarter than that."

"I don't disagree but I'm not the problem."

"Henrietta Boyle."

"She's ambitious, Pathologically so and this movie star case just fell into her lap. She's not going to let go even if she has to drop the gas pellets on Taylor personally."

"She took an oath, for God's sake," I say.

"I know but people like her can be corrupted by things beside money. She's driven by the need for power. It consumes her and it blinds her."

"Fill her in."

"She won't listen."

"Then go over her head."

A pause and then he says, "I'm not prepared to do that. Not yet."

"All right, fill her in anyway and see what happens."

"I'll try," Hayes says with little conviction.

"Meanwhile, I may returning to Los Angeles in the next couple of days and I wanted to make sure you kept in touch with Chief Bridger."

"I will. Definitely. Safe trip."

"Thanks," I say and hang up.

I heat up my coffee from the carafe and check my watch. Bunny should be back at the office by now unless she lingered to gab with some of the local pols or maybe one or two advertisers. She's been known to do that and she's good at it. I resign myself to patience and turn my attention back to the newspaper spread. More squinting and then, frustrated, I dig into my wallet and dig out a business card and place a call to the Santa Rosa Press-Democrat. When I get though I ask for Gracie James and am told by the editor that she's on assignment. The filming at Bodega Bay? That's right. I thank him and hang up, then place a call to Norman Deming.

"You again?" he growls but only for effect.

"Me," I say. "I'm looking for Gracie James. Is she around?"

"Not exactly. She's up in the chopper that's taking aerial shots of the town and the bay for the process plates. You want her to call you?"

"Please," I say. I give him the number at the Inn.

"How's it coming?" Deming asks.

"Making progress, Norm. Rod may be able to travel back with you Sunday."

"Remind me to kiss you when next I see you," he says.

"Remind me to duck," I reply and hang up.

The next half hour crawls by interminably. If I didn't know

better I'd suspect Bunny of having a nooner but of course, she isn't. Not my Bunny. As for Gracie, it feels like she must be flying to San Diego. The phone rings. I avoid my previous mistake.

"Who's this?" I ask.

"Gracie. Is that you, Joe?"

"It is. Happy to hear you're back safely on the ground."

"It was a gas. So what's up?"

"I need your help. I assume you've got proofs and negs on everything you've taken at the bay."

"You bet."

"There's one shot I need to see up close."

"Well, everything's back at my place in Santa Rosa."

"Oh," I say, deflated.

"I'm heading for home in about ten minutes if you want to meet me there."

I brighten up immediately.

"You bet," I say.

She gives me directions to her address and her phone number in case I get lost or delayed. I tell her I'm in Palo Alto, maybe forty minutes away,. She says she'll be home long before that. After hanging up, I grab the Palo Alto newspaper and head out. As I turn onto 101 heading north toward San Francisco, I remember my call to Bunny. She will call the room and then she will call again and then again and some time in the near future I'm going to hear about this. Oh, am I going to hear.

# CHAPTER EIGHTEEN

I find Gracie's house with little trouble. It's a small two-bedroom ranch on a small lot showing slight signs of neglect. Maybe that's thanks to her one-time live-in who moved out on her a couple of months ago. Her car's in the driveway and sure enough, when I ring the doorbell she opens the door immediately with a smile.

"Didn't get lost, I see," she says.

"Even I couldn't screw up your directions," I say as she steps aside inviting me in. She offers me something to drink. I pass and hand her the Palo Alto paper, pointing out the wharf-building photo.

"I remember that one," she nods. "Nice fellas. Locals."

"Do you know who they are? There's no caption."

She smiles. "I always take names, Joe. What kind of a photographer do you think I am? Come on."

She leads me down a short hallway into what was once the second bedroom and ushers me in. The first thing I notice is that all the windows have been painted black. The second thing is the amount of equipment which has been crammed into very few square feet. Against one wall is a sink and work area. Opposite is a table with a printer and an enlarger and more work space. Alongside are maybe a dozen filing cabinets and the rest of the wall space is taken up by floor to ceiling shelving. Four thin wires holding clothes pins stretch from one side of the room to another. A bunch of glossies have been drying there all day and Gracie snaps them down and stacks them on a shelf. A quick second glance at the newspaper photo and she opens a drawer and takes out a sheaf of glossies. Quickly she thumbs through them until she finds what I'm looking for. She turns it over and reads: "Building a prop wharf at the Gaffney house. Harv Edwards, Kiwi Parsons and Patrick Hannigan."

Hannigan? I've heard that name before.

"Hannigan? You're sure?"

"Sure I'm sure," she says handing me the 8 x 10 glossy. That's what it says, all right. Patrick Hannigan. Now I remember Norm Deming mentioning him. A local who gave his address as the old folks home and then disappeared after three days without picking up his pay. I flip the photo over and study the face. The image is much larger than what was in the paper but there's a shadow partially obscuring his features and also something written on his tee shirt which I can't quite make out. I point it out to Gracie.

"Can you enlarge this section right here?" I ask.

"No problem," she says as she digs back into the drawer and takes out a roll of exposed negative. Ten minutes later she hands me the print. Now there's no doubt in my mind. The half-face that I can make out belongs to Hank Perry, I'm sure of it. As for the tee shirt, the letters FOO stand out clearly as do the letters below, CO. The rest of the shirt is in shadow but again, I have no doubts. Foothill College.

"Do you have anything else from this site? Maybe something closer on this man?"

She shakes her head.

"That's all I've got. I remember I was in a hurry. We were losing the light."

"But you'd recognize him if you saw him again."

"I think so."

170

"I need to use your phone."

"Go ahead."

"Long distance."

"Mars?"

"Texas."

"That won't break me."

I get the number for Baylor University from information and ask to be connected. It's late Friday. Half past five. The business office may be closed. I hope not. I get lucky. A pleasant female voice answers the phone and I ask to be connected to the athletic department. It takes five rings but a basso named Conklin picks up. He's the backfield coach for the football team and says he knows diddely about the golf program but when I press him, he assures me that no alumni golf tournament was held at the school this month, last month or any other month for that matter. I thank him and hang up, then look at Gracie.

"One more call," I say. "Closer to home."

It's a few minutes to seven and we have hastily gathered in the office of Henrietta Boyle, Assistant D.A. for Sonoma County. Me, Gracie, Sergeant Hayes and the lady herself. I hand her the photo.

"This is him," I say, jabbing a finger at Hank Perry. "This is your killer."

She looks intently, checks the back.

"His name is Hank Perry," I say. "He was hired by the movie company using the name Patrick Hannigan."

"You have proof of this, Mr. Bernardi?" Boyle asks.

"Let me take you through it."

And I do. Slowly and carefully. Amanda Broome, heiress, due to inherit millions within a matter of weeks. Constance Perry, executrix of the estate, who probably killed her wealthy brother thirteen years ago and has been managing his fortune ever since. She stands to lose everything when Amanda comes of age. Roy Perry,

171

an underpaid school teacher who has been blackmailing his ex-wife for years. He, too, stands to lose a great deal of money when Amanda reaches her 21st birthday. And Hank Perry, the pampered son who has never been refused anything by a doting father, he, too, is in danger of having the spigot shut off. But unlike his father and Constance, I believe Hank had been staying in touch with Amanda. One or two phone calls a month, I would guess. No one with Hank Perry's mindset would cast an heiress out of his life, it would be sacrilege. Amanda probably told him about the restraining order Rod Taylor took out and from the newspaper publicity prior to the filming in Bodega Bay Hank knew that Taylor would be on the scene, a perfect patsy for a murder scheme which would draw attention away from the inheritance, normally the first and most logical and maybe the only place the authorities would look."

I raise my voice slightly on this last part, speaking with emphasis as I look Henrietta Boyle in the eye. To her credit, she does not look away.

"Proof, Mr. Bernardi. I'm still waiting," she says.

"Bear with me. He calls Amanda, knowing she, as wild and unbalanced as she is, will race north to confront Taylor. Once the angry scene in the hotel lobby takes place, all that remains is to slit her throat and dump her body into the trunk of Taylor's car. The next day he disappears, gets himself to the San Francisco airport where he appears to have deplaned from Texas and is met by his father after having competed in a golf tournament that never took place."

"More speculation, Mr. Bernardi," Boyle says.

"Yes," I say, "but what delicious speculation, ma'am. It hangs together so well and even more to the point, it makes a lot more sense than a vicious murder committed by a well-known film actor who has just had a violent confrontation with the victim in a hotel lobby, witnessed by dozens onlookers, who then, in a fit of gross stupidity, slits her throat and stows her body in the trunk of his own car. That alone could get him an acquittal on the grounds of insanity. Did I forget to mention, Miz Boyle, you have no witnesses, no fingerprints, no forensic evidence of any kind and frankly, I like my speculation a lot better than yours."

"So do I," Sergeant Hayes says. "If we can make a positive ID that this Perry kid was at the Bodega filming site working with an alias, I think we can make a case that a grand jury will buy."

"I disagree," Boyle says. "I want you to keep directing your efforts in Mr. Taylor's direction."

"That will be a waste of time," Hayes says.

"That is an order, Sergeant."

"Ma'am, I do not take orders from the District Attorney's office, I take orders from my Captain."

"Then I'll have a talk with your Captain," she says coldly.

"And maybe I'll have a talk with your boss, the District Attorney," Hayes says getting to his feet.

Boyle glares at him.

"Sergeant, you are insubordinate and churlish."

"No, ma'am, just doing my job like you should be doing yours. You'll excuse me."

He strides to the door and walks out, shutting the door behind him.

Five minutes later Gracie and I catch up with him in the parking lot, pacing and smoking a cigarette.

"Bitch," he mutters angrily. Then, "Sorry, ma'am."

"I've heard the word before," Gracie says.

"Stupid woman's got the Governor's mansion on the brain and she thinks your friend is her ticket. Hollywood star arrested in brutal slaying, D.A. promises quick conviction. Her name and face splattered over every newspaper in the state, television interviews, maybe even Long John Nebel, for God's sake. The woman has no shame."

"I'll call Ezra tonight," I say. "He'll call the District Attorney. That might turn her around."

"I doubt it. She's planning to run against him this November."

"Great. So what's next?" I ask.

Gracie pipes up. "How about it if we go to the golf tournament tomorrow? I'll eyeball the guy and if he's the one in the photo, I'll let you know."

I look at Hayes. Hayes looks at Gracie and shrugs.

"It's a start," he says.

It's just past nine when I get back to Palo Alto and call Ezra Crabtree. He listens intently with few interruptions as I lay everything out for him.

"This is good, Joe. Very good," Ezra says. "You and Sergeant Hayes are right. This makes a lot more sense than Henrietta Boyle's wet dream about convicting Mr. Taylor. First thing in the morning I'll call the D.A. Henrietta screwing up will make his day. Hell, he might even fire her. I think he's been looking for an excuse."

After talking to Ezra I call Chief Bridger at home and repeat what I told Ezra. He, too, sees the logic of what we've got although he cautions that most of it is circumstantial. I tell him I'm well aware of the fact.

"So, tomorrow morning you're driving to San Francisco to this golf tournament," Bridger says.

"I'm meeting Gracie and Sergeant Hayes there at ten o'clock."

"I want to be in on this, Joe. Come by the office at nine-thirty. I'll drive."

"Better you than me, Chief. The rattles in the Bentley are getting louder."

He laughs.

The bed is comfortable, the room is cool but I get a lousy night's sleep. Maybe it's because Bunny isn't lying next to me or maybe it's the anticipation of finally putting this case to rest. Whatever the reason, I toss and turn and finally at six o'clock I am awake for good and spend an hour staring at the ceiling until at last my stomach grumbles me out of bed in search of breakfast.

The Olympic Club is a venerable institution in San Francisco. An athletic club as well as a social club, it goes back a hundred years and is headquartered at Union Square although its golf facilities are located some distance south bordering on Daly City. It boasts three courses—Lake and Ocean which are traditional and Cliff which is a par 3. Today and Sunday the Lake Course will host the California Open and when Chief Bridger and I get within a couple of blocks of the clubhouse, it's clear that a good sized crowd has already begun to gather. Traffic cones are funneling private cars to a nearby vacant field where volunteers of both sexes and all ages supervise the parking. A dozen busses from nearby communities are stacked up off to the side and rotating shuttle busses are transporting fans to the main entrance to the course. Tickets are on sale at six dollars each. Bridger shows his badge but in vain. Six bucks, please. No exceptions. I'm wealthy. I pay for us both. As we walk in I see Gracie and Hayes waving to us and we hurry toward them. Hayes is in uniform. Probably tried to pull the same dodge Bridger did. I spot a nearby leaderboard. H. Perry is listed in fourth place at three under par.

"I asked the starter," Hayes tells us. "He says Perry should be around the seventh hole by now." He consults his course layout and points. "That way." We start off on the cart path, weaving our way through the crowds. It's warm and clear and a perfect day for golf. The atmosphere is festive.

We are almost to the seventh tee box when I spot Roy Perry and he spots me. A strange look crosses his face. Concern, maybe. Perhaps panic. He hurries toward us.

"Mr. Bernardi. Chief. What are you doing here?"

"We need to talk to Hank," I say. About twenty yards away a

threesome is putting out on the sixth green. One of them looks like Hank but from this distance I can't be sure.

"This really isn't the time," Roy Perry says.

"Sorry, Professor," Bridger says, "but I'm afraid this is the time." He starts to look around. By now Perry is in full panic mode.

"Look, whatever you need to know, I can answer your questions," he says.

"About what?" Bridger asks.

"Everything," Perry says, "Let's go over there. It's less crowded." He points to a shaded spot on the edge of a heavily wooded area, He, Bridger, Hayes and I walk over, out of earshot of the crowds.

"Well?" Bridger says.

"You were right. That Saturday, I did drive to town and I did borrow that car."

"And while you were borrowing it without permission, Doctor, you did try to kill me," I say coldly.

"I'd hoped it wouldn't come to that. I'm not a violent man but I was afraid. Afraid because you were getting too close."

"Too close to what?" Bridger asks.

"My arrangement with Constance."

"You mean blackmail," I say.

"Call it that if you like," he says, annoyed.

"I like," Bridger says. "So Constance Perry, your ex-wife, killed her brother."

"Yes."

"You witnessed it?"

"As good as," he says.

"Suppose you tell us," Bridger says.

"I was driving over to see Andrew, to borrow money. It was the night he died. I didn't like doing it. I'd never asked before but at that time I had no choice. Universities give golf scholarships, elementary schools don't. Hank had been accepted by this very fine, very well known private school but they were demanding his tuition be paid before the next term started and I was tapped out. I was approaching Andrew's place—it was about nine o'clock—when this car came from the opposite direction. It turned into the driveway and I recognized it immediately. It belonged to Isobel Graham. I pulled to the side of the road and cut my lights. Even though I was some distance away I could see both Isobel and Constance get out of the car and go inside. Back then I was one of the few people who knew what their relationship really was."

"But there must have been talk," I say.

"Some. Not much. Most of it was dismissed as sleaze without substance. I should have gone home then and there but I had to have the money and I was damned if I was going to ask for it in front of either Constance or Isobel. So I sat and I waited and a half hour went by and suddenly I heard two shots being fired from within the house. I got out of my car and raced to the gates, punched in the code—Andrew had given it to me months before- and ran up the driveway to the house. Before I got to the front door I glanced in the window to the study and there was Isobel, positioning the body on the floor, and Constance with her mallet and chisel marking up the exterior of the wall safe to make it look like a burglary gone wrong. I turned around, raced back down the driveway and drove home. The next day Andrew's murder was page one on all the local papers and the lead on the television news broadcasts. The official story, which I'm sure you are familiar with, was a total fabrication. Late in the afternoon, I called Constance and invited her for dinner. She refused, of course, until I told her what I had seen through the window the night before. I suggested she bring Isobel along and she did so as well as bringing a .38 caliber revolver. I was waiting for her with a .45 automatic and a carbon copy of a letter I had put into my safe deposit box that afternoon in an envelope marked "To be opened in the event of my death no matter what the apparent cause."

"Very slick," Bridger says.

"And very safe."

"And your son Hank knew nothing of this?"

"He believed the extra money each month was some sort of unofficial alimony. So, if you would like me to return with you to Palo Alto, Chief, I place myself in your hands."

"I still have to talk to your son, Doctor Perry," Bridger says. By now Gracie, who had lingered at the tee box, has returned to the group. I look at her quizzically.

"It's him, Mr. Bernardi," she says. "It's Patrick Hannigan."

"Hannigan? What are you talking about?" Perry says.

"There's another matter that has to be dealt with, Doctor," Bridger says, "and that is the murder of Amanda Broome."

"Hank knows nothing about that," Perry says.

"That remains to be seen," Bridger says.

"Where is he now, Gracie?" Hayes asks.

"They just hit their balls and are walking up the fairground. Perry sliced one into the woods on the left."

I shake my head.

"That's a hook, not a slice, Gracie," I say.

She shrugs.

"So? The only time I ever played golf I was hitting the ball through little windmills."

"Let's go talk to young Mr. Perry," Bridger says and we start up the path alongside the seventh fairway. Up ahead the crowd seems to have congregated in an area by the woods and a couple of marshals are trying to keep order. When we arrive the spectators are abuzz.

"What's going on?" I ask a nearby man carrying binoculars.

"I think he's gone."

"What?"

"Hank Perry. He went into the woods to find his ball and he

just kept going. Somebody said he jogged across the next fairway toward the highway. Now what the hell would make him do a thing like that?"

# CHAPTER NINETEEN

We head for the parking lot, Roy Perry in tow, and convoy south to Palo Alto. Gracie leads in her car, next comes the Cadillac with Perry behind the wheel and Sergeant Hayes in the passenger seat. Chief Bridger and I bring up the rear. On the way, Bridger radios a description of Hank Perry to the county sheriff's office as well as the Highway Patrol requesting an APB (All Points Bulletin). Perry is alone and on foot, his car having been left in the contestant's parking area. Until Bridger can arrange to have it towed, it sports a spiffy looking Denver boot on the right rear tire. Within minutes law enforcement units across the state will be on the alert. Bridger thinks he'll be caught within a matter of hours. On foot and with only the money in his wallet he can't go far.

When we arrive at police headquarters in Palo Alto, Roy Perry is booked on three charges: car theft, reckless endangerment and attempted murder, all three of which he has copped to in front of witnesses. The issue of blackmail will have to wait until Constance and Isobel are interrogated. Unless Perry is lying, the two women face major charges of their own.

Eventually Perry is brought into the Chief's office where Bridger and I are waiting for him. Gracie and Sergeant Hayes are on their way back to Santa Rosa. Hayes is anxious to report the morning's events to Assistant District Attorney Boyle. You might think of that as rubbing her nose in it. You wouldn't be far wrong. Bridger gestures to a chair. Perry takes a seat.

"I must tell you, Professor," Bridger says, "that I am profoundly disappointed in your behavior. A man of your learning with your credentials to find himself involved in this sordid mess, it is a sad and degrading situation."

Perry says nothing, staring at the floor. What can he say? Bridger is right. An enormously gifted man has thrown his life away and for what? An ingrate of a son who in all likelihood is a cold blooded killer? Shakespeare would have made a damned good play of this.

"I am not going to lock you up, Dr. Perry," Bridger says. Perry's head snaps up, looking at him in disbelief. "Given your status in the community, I don't feel you are a flight risk so I am releasing you on your own recognizance."

"Thank you, Chief Bridger," Perry says. "That is extremely generous of you."

"But you are not to leave the area and you are to check in with this office at least once a day. You will be notified of your court date and failure to appear will result in the issuance of a fugitive warrant. Given the seriousness of the charges against you and those to come, you do not want to make your situation more desperate."

"I understand."

"All right then, you are free to go. And Doctor, you don't need me to advise you to get yourself a lawyer. A very good lawyer."

"Yes, of course," he says and then hurries out the door.

I stare at Bridger, puzzled and almost amused.

"Thanks," I say.

"You're welcome," Bridger responds. "For what?"

"Considering that I'm the aggrieved party, you might have given me a heads up before releasing the rat from his trap."

Bridger smiles as he picks up the phone and punches a number on his intercom pad. A moment later he is talking to a subordinate

"Chet, I just released Perry on O.R. I want him followed around the clock starting immediately, home and office, and first thing Monday morning, apply to Judge Ransom for a phone tap. Same deal. Home and office and don't worry about the overtime. Thanks." He hangs up and looks over at me. "Hank Perry's on the run, broke, without transportation and probably scared out of his mind. He's going to contact the one person who has been enabling him all his life. When he does we'll snatch him up. Any questions?"

"None," I say. "Forgive my stupidity."

"Not stupid, Joe, but this is what I do. Anyway, you've taken this about as far as you can and your contribution is much appreciated but it's in my hands now. What are your plans?"

"Not sure. Probably head back to Bodega Bay. I think the company's moving back to the studio tomorrow, maybe Monday, and I'm pretty sure Taylor's going with them. I'll touch base with Ezra."

Bridger gets up and comes around his desk to shake my hand.

"Some time in the future we may need you back here to testify. Leave your phone number with the desk sergeant and be sure to call me before you head south. I'll try to keep you apprised of what's going on."

"I'd appreciate it," I say.

"There were a few harsh words between us, Joe, best forgotten. No hard feelings?"

"None on my part."

"Good," he says walking me to the door. "Safe trip."

I collect the Bentley from the parking lot and head for the Burgundy where I need to make a couple of phone calls before checking out. Bridger is right. I'm pretty much done here. Chances are excellent that Rod is now in the clear and that the evidence against Hank Perry will start to pile up. I don't feel sorry for the kid, far from it, but I can understand the desperation he must have felt when he realized that his soft and privileged life style was about to implode. No more cash from Constance Perry, no more country club, no more dallying with the likes of Gloria Weidemeyer and the other nubile little rich girls of the Los Altos Hills gentry. His father had prepared him for everything except real life which was suddenly slapping him in the face.

My first call is to Ezra who has heard from Gracie and Sergeant Hayes and in turn, he has called Rod to fill him in. Henrietta Boyle is backing away from her earlier stance as fast as her stumpy legs will take her. Ezra says she hasn't been fired but she's on a tight leash. As soon as I hang up I call Norm Deming. He tells me that the location shoot will wrap around supper time this evening. Tomorrow the company heads south to Universal City. I ask him to do me a favor, to have someone go to my room, pack my suitcase and bring it to the studio where I'll pick it up Monday. Then I call the front desk and ask them to send the bill for our stay to my home address. I'll drop a check in the mail immediately. I have realized that no good purpose is served in returning to Bodega Bay which is an hour in the wrong direction. I don't need the wear and tear. Neither does my ailing car.

I check my watch. Quarter to one. I really should get going but my eyes are heavy from last night's lack of sleep. I decide to stretch out on the bed for a couple of hours before starting the drive home. I estimate seven hours max to the house. If I leave at three I'll be at my front door by ten. It sounds like a plan. I leave a wake up call with the desk, kick off my shoes, scrunch my head atop the pillow, curl up and try to think good thoughts.

A short time later the phone rings. Groggily I reach over and lift the receiver. "Thank you," I say, about to hang up, when I hear Bridger's voice.

"Thank you for what?"

"Chief?"

"Is Roy Perry there with you?"

"No, why should he be?"

"He's in the wind, Joe. We've lost him."

"What happened?"

"He pulled out of his driveway around twelve-thirty, headed for town. My guys were on him about ten lengths back. In the middle of traffic they got caught at a light and Perry ducked down an alley. By the time they got there, he was gone."

"Shit," I mutter.

"Sorry to have bothered you, Joe. Again, have a safe trip."

"Wait!" I say before he can disconnect. "Can't go, Chief. Not now. I need to see the I's dotted and the T's crossed."

"Forget it, Joe. We'll have him by suppertime. Go see your wife."

"I'll see my wife when they're both locked up. Call me back here at the inn."

"If it'll make you happy," he says and hangs up.

No, it won't make me happy. In fact I'm very UNhappy but I'm damned if I am going to leave before the package is wrapped, taped, ribboned and fitted with a bow. I call the coffee shop and order chocolate cake, strawberry shortcake and coffee. This is either lunch or supper, I don't know which and I really don't care. I am totally aware that I'm losing my mind but I don't care about that either.

It's quarter past four when the phone rings. I have been sitting in the easy chair dozing. Bridger, I think. He has news. Or maybe not. I lift the receiver.

"Tell me," I say.

"Joe?"

I recognize the voice and it isn't Chief Bridger. It's Roy Perry.

"Where are you, Doctor Perry?"

"At a motel in Redwood City. I want to turn myself in but I can't call Bridger. After running out on him, he'll send the whole damned trigger-happy police department after me."

"I doubt that. Where's Hank, Doc? Where's your son?"

There's a moment's hesitation. Then he says, "Here with me. Will you come, Joe?"

"Not without Bridger, I won't," I tell him. "I've already been to that party up in the hills above Bodega Bay. Remember?"

Another hesitation.

"All right, just Bridger then. You and Bridger. No one else."

"Okay. What's the name of this place?"

"The Maddux Motel on Kensington Road close to Maddux Park. Room 121. I'd suggest you send an ambulance but I think it's a little late for that."

"What? What do you mean by that? Doc?"

"By Maddux Park. You can't miss it."

He hangs up. I splash cold water in my face, comb my hair and head for the parking lot.

Bridger is angry.

"What the hell is he calling you for? Doesn't he trust me?"

"He's not thinking straight. I could hear it in his voice."

Bridger grunts and reaches for the phone on his desk.

"I'll have the Redwood City police pick him up," he says.

"No!" I say quickly. "He's expecting me. Me and you. Anybody else shows up, God knows what might happen. We need answers, Chief, not more corpses."

He lowers the phone.

"Yeah, you're right. I'll drive."

Redwood City is about fifteen miles south of the golf course, maybe six miles north of Palo Alto. Bridger is grim faced as he cruises 101 at more than 70 miles an hour, lights flashing all the way. I've seen Bridger, the politician, and Bridger, the smart cop. Now I'm looking over at a man with pride who doesn't like being toyed with. Maybe the professor was right to call me first.

The motel is easy to find and we glide into the parking lot, lights no longer flashing. Room 121 is at ground level with an outside entrance to the room. Bridger knocks. Almost immediately Roy Perry opens the door. His face is drawn and pale. He looks behind us for signs of additional police, then steps aside to let us go in.

Bridger doesn't have to ask where Hank is. We see him as soon as we enter the room. He's lying on the floor, sightless eyes staring at the ceiling, a pool of congealing blood visible beneath his head. Bridger kneels down beside him and feels for a pulse but it's only procedural. We both know he's dead. The lack of pulse confirms it.

"I tried to revive him," Perry says. "I couldn't. I guess I knew right away he was dead."

Bridger gets to his feet and goes to the closet where he takes down an extra blanket and covers Hank's body. He looks back at Perry.

"What happened here, Doctor?"

"I killed him. I killed my son," Perry says, shaking and choking on the words.

"Calm down and take it slow. Start at the beginning. How did you get here?"

Perry lowers himself onto the bed while I settle into a straight chair by the writing desk. Bridger remains standing.

"Even as I was walking in my front door," Perry says, "the phone was ringing. It was Hank. He was crying, scared to death. He begged me to help him. I asked him what was going on. He said he'd tell me when he saw me. He told me where he was and asked me to bring him money. I told him it was Saturday. The banks were closed. I had maybe a couple of hundred dollars in the house. He said that would have to be enough and gave directions to this motel.

"I pulled out of the driveway and right away I spotted your men, Chief. They were pretty obvious. I drove to Palo Alto to blend in with the Saturday shopping crowd and managed to give your officers the slip. It didn't take me long to get to Redwood City and find this place. As I said Hank was a mess, babbling, making no sense. He said as soon as he saw the woman from the filming at Bodega Bay that the police were onto him. That's why the cop was with her, so that he could make the arrest. I told Hank to slow down. What woman ? What filming? Arrest him for what? He said, I did it, Pop. They know I did it but I had to, don't you see? For both of us. I couldn't let the little bitch inherit all that money. By that time I was getting angry. Hank was incoherent. I said, did what? What did you do, Hank? He looked at me as if I were some kind of fool. I killed her, Pop. I had to. It was the only way.

"I couldn't believe what he was saying? He'd killed Amanda? No, never. Not my boy. I didn't bring him up that way. He kept saying he had to. We needed the money. We had to have it. I told him he was wrong, that we'd never really "needed" it. We'd have survived without it. I told him he had to turn himself into the police. He shook his head violently. Never, he said. We'd both go to prison, him for Amanda and me for the blackmail. I said I didn't care what happened to me but maybe a good lawyer could get him off or get him a lighter sentence. He just laughed and demanded the money I'd brought. I refused. He said he needed the money as well as the car, that he was going to drive north and cross the border into Canada. Lots of kids were doing it these days, young guys like him who wanted no part of the army or Viet Nam. I refused again and he grabbed me and threw me to the floor and started clawing for my wallet and keys. I tried to fight back but he was young and strong, a lot stronger than me."

Perry falls silent for a moment staring down at the floor. I look at Bridger who is grim-faced. He walks over to the dresser and pours a glass of water from a pitcher and hands it to Perry who takes it gratefully. He drinks and hands back the glass.

"I'd done everything for him, given him whatever he wanted or needed, everything except a mother. Maybe he secretly resented me for that, I don't know. He headed for the door with the money and my car keys. I struggled to my feet, grabbed him, tried to drag him back into the room. He tried to throw me off but I wouldn't let him and I pushed him and he stumbled backwards, hitting his head on the corner of that dresser. I heard him grunt in pain and he went limp and fell at my feet. I knelt down, searched for a pulse, then tried artificial respiration. Before long I gave up. Looking into his sightless eyes I knew he was dead. I was in a panic. I didn't know what to do. That's when I called you, Mr. Bernardi."

I look over at Bridger. His expression is still grim but I think I see flecks of compassion in his eyes. He walks over to the telephone and dials the Redwood City police.

# CHAPTER TWENTY

Nine days have passed. I've been home a week. The first thing I did was take the Bentley to Reggie, my service guy. He looked at the nicks and scrapes to the body and declared the situation minor. Then he turned the key in the ignition and his cheery disposition changed to nervous apprehension. That's why I am now driving around in a 1960 Morris Minor Woody Wagon which is a feat of British automotive engineering as long as you don't try to drive it up a hill. Reggie says he's sure he can have the Bentley back to me by the end of the month which is disheartening since today is the 3rd. Even with the driver's seat in the fully back position, my legs are threatening to secede from my body if the situation doesn't improve.

Bunny is delighted to have me home and shows it in every way possible. Yvette made a huge fuss when I first walked through the door, but now I am just the man that she and Mommy Bunny have dinner with every night. I have learned that Yvette has discovered, and has been discovered by, a boy that lives five doors down from us. Question. Is there some switch that little girls have hidden inside their brains that activates when they turn 9 or 10 and transforms the cells into incoherent mush? I have a dreadful premonition that my life is about to take a turn and not for the better.

The news about the Bodega Bay murder has slowed to a trickle after an initial maelstrom that was picked up by the press nationwide. Rod Taylor is now a bona fide victim of evil forces determined to destroy his career. Half the reporters and columnists, the ones who had been so quick to pillory him, now reveal that they felt all along that he was being set up for a murder he didn't commit. How could I have misjudged them so? The spotlight has now swung over to Constance Perry and her very good friend, Isobel Graham, both of whom may soon be charged in the 13 year old death of Andrew Broome. Even better the press has a juicier story to pursue. Three days ago an adulterous U.S. Senator pushed Rod and the film off the front pages. The weepy betrayed wife made great copy. The sexy slinky adulteress made even better copy and no story was printed anywhere without at least one lascivious photograph to spice up the text.

I have been in constant contact with Jerry Kaplan about the progress of our movie. Almost everything is right on track, he'd told me a couple of days ago. His partner Pat Brady was on the road, firming up locations, arranging for catering, and all the other niggling little details that need tending to in the production of a major motion picture. Sensing that I wasn't being told the whole story, I'd asked him to be more specific about that phrase 'almost everything'.

"What about Piper?" I'd wanted to know. No problem, he'd told me. Signed and sealed and ready to go. Two years ago Piper Laurie was nominated for an Academy Award for her role in 'The Hustler', having put into mothballs a wasted decade of meaningless roles in brainless comedies or insulting sand and sandals epics in which she wore scanty outfits and regurgitated banal dialogue. But strangely, nothing happened on the heels of her nomination and she moved out of Hollywood back to New York. Now she is going to play Jessie, Walt's love interest, and I couldn't be more delighted. Neither can Piper who loves the script.

"Okay," I'd said. "Piper's on board. Explain 'almost everything'."

He hesitates. I know Jerry. The longer this takes to get out, the worse it's going to be. A full ten seconds pass. If I were the President I would go to DefCom One immediately.

"Columbia backed out, Joe."

"Oh, crap," I'd said. Columbia was putting up half the money and handling distribution. This was a major blow.

"Not to worry," Jerry had told me. "I've made a deal with Allied Artists."

My heart had sunk. Losing Columbia was bad enough. Allied Artists was basically Monogram pictures reborn. True, they'd released a few good pictures but most of their product was Grade D quickie programmers for the bottom end of double features.

"And the money?"

"Less."

Less? We were already on a no-calorie budget.

"How much less?"

"Well, Pat's in Bakersfield. We're going to try to double it for the Oklahoma oil fields. Also the Sierras for the Rockies and the Sacramento River for the Missouri."

"And what are we going to use to double Mt. Rushmore?"

"The Mt. Rushmore sequence is out, Joe. We'll need a rewrite."

"Great. And Rod Taylor?"

"We haven't heard from his manager. Joe, but I'm sure there's no problem. By the way Allied wants you to take a producer credit on the picture."

"What picture is that?" I'd asked snidely.

"We're not dead yet. Pat and I, we're nobodies. Allied seems to think your name will mean something to the exhibitors. I agree."

I barely heard what he was saying. I couldn't get Rod out of my mind, sensing a betrayal after all I had gone through for the man. When I'd hung up, I'd been totally depressed. We always knew the picture would be low budget, that Wendkos would have to shoot fast and shoot good, but it suddenly felt as if the Fates were conspiring against us. Well, today I'm going to find out because Rod has asked me to join him for lunch at the Universal commissary. Either he's in or he's out and before the day is over, I'll know which it is.

I drive up to the Lankershim entrance around a quarter of twelve. Scotty, the gate guard, smiles a hello, perhaps amused by my car. He slips a drive-on pass under my windshield wiper and suggests I park next to Stage 10 which is idle but close to Stage 12 where Hitchcock is filming.

The light over the stage door is unlit so I walk in. The crew is bustling about getting ready for the next setup. I spot Bob Burks, the DP, who waves to me. I wave back. Several of the crew give me a quick muffled hello as they go about their business. I spot Hitch sitting in his camp chair, the camera directly behind him, focused on what appears to be an attic. He's talking to the assistant director who is kneeling beside him and nodding. Off to one side I see Tippi Hedren being tended to by hair and makeup. Her hair is frazzled and her face is blotched with red marks and traces of blood. She is quiet and staring straight ahead and I can tell she is upset.

The A.D. stands. "First team," he calls out. This means, all actors in the upcoming shot, take your places. In this case it means just Tippi. She walks into the set and takes her place by a closed door. The second assistant with the clacker holds it up in front of the camera. Scene 144. Take 15.

"And action," Hitch says and suddenly Tippi is backing up against the door, trying to shield her face and eyes, terrified, as crows and blackbirds attack her. Most are harmless stuffed birds which are thrown in her direction by crew members but several of the birds are real and they are pecking at her, cutting into her skin and I realize that Tippi isn't acting, she is genuinely terrified.

"Cut," Hitchcock says. "Again. Right away, please."

The second assistant wipes off the 15 and writes in 16. A moment later they go again and I wonder what the hell is going through Hitchcock's mind. Sixteen takes and he isn't satisfied as his star gets assaulted and in real danger of losing an eye. I try to picture Bergman or Grace Kelly sitting still for this kind of treatment and I can't. Tippi, newcomer that she is, has no power to fight back. I wonder what she has done, or perhaps not done, to provoke such treatment at Hitchcock's hands. I've heard stories about his obsessiveness, very possibly sexual in nature, but I had never believed them. Now I am not so sure.

"Cut," Hitch says.

"Reset for closeup," says the A.D. and Tippi makes her way back to her camp chair while the camera crew adjusts the lights and the lenses.

I feel a hand clap me on the shoulder and turn to find Rod smiling at me.

"Gruesome,eh?" he says.

"Very," I respond.

"It's what Hitch calls the money shot. It's what the picture's all about."

"Really? Hard to believe."

"I've made reservations at the Smokehouse," he says. "My car's right by the door. I'll drive."

"No commissary?"

"For you, Joe? Never," he grins."And I'm buying."

The Smokehouse is an upscale eatery located in Burbank and only minutes by car from Universal, Warner Bros. and the Disney Studios. Executives frequent it, some on a daily basis, and usually you can find a star or two and some not-quite-stars at a table trying to attract attention. Rod has booked us a table in a secluded corner where we can talk quietly without being overheard. As for attracting attention he says he's had quite enough of that for the past couple of weeks. We order a couple of beers and pretend to scan the menu. I suspect we both know it by heart.

"So what did you think about that scene they were filming with Tippi?" I ask him.

"Vintage Hitchcock," he replies.

"Don't let Hitch hear you say that."

"Oh?"

"Evan Hunter says that Hitch is tired of being looked upon as a genre director. He wants to do something meaningful and he thinks this may be it."

"Meaningful?" Rod shakes his head. "I don't know about that. This is a people-pleasing thriller about birds gone berserk and Hitch doesn't even attempt to explain why. Meaningful? No."

"Maybe it's his matchup with John Ford in the Oscar parade that's got him yearning for critical respectability. Ford 4, Hitchcock 0."

"Maybe but since when did Pappy ever pretend to be making art, even though he was?"

"Point taken," I say.

The waiter comes by and takes our order and as he walks away, Rod reaches in his pocket and takes out some folded papers and hands them to me. I glance at them. It's his contract for our picture. I flip to the last page. It's unsigned. I look up at him curiously.

"I'm sorry, Joe," Rod says. "You're too good a friend to fob off with a phone call or worse, letting my manager handle it. If there were any way I could make this work, I would but I can't. Piper Laurie. My God, do you know how fabulous that is? She is going to be wonderful. I would kill to be working with her. I'm sick about this, I really am."

"Tell me."

"Ten years ago I was working for a Sydney department store, designing and staging window displays for a living and working in little theater for no money trying to get a career going. I got a small part in a low budget film about one of my ancestors and it did well and I got good notices and this film producer looked me up and made me what I thought was a pretty good deal. Three pictures at better than scale and he'd pay me up front for all of them. I jumped at it. We made two. They were okay but nothing to get excited about. In '54 I won an award and got a ticket to London via Los Angeles. I asked the producer about the third picture. He said he'd let me know and to go with God. I took the flight and got off in L.A. and found myself an agent. You know the rest."

"And now this producer has the third picture ready for you," I say, hazarding a guess.

He nods. "I asked him to put it off. He said he couldn't do that, that he had commitments. The truth is, he wants to make this picture and release it at the same time as 'The Birds' to cash in on a Hitchcock film. He's got a lawyer and promises to sue me for everything I have if I don't comply."

"We can wait," I say.

"I'm not sure you can, Joe. I've already signed to do 'The VIPs" with Taylor and Burton in the fall. We had this window but now it's no longer there. My manager talked to Jerry first thing this morning. You're locked into a bunch of locations. Piper and a couple of other performers have play or pay contracts. You've got a start date in three weeks and you're stuck with it."

I look away. This is a blow to my gut and I don't know what to do about it. Rod's watching me carefully and I sense that he may feel worse about this than I do.

"I was looking forward to playing Walt, I really was, Joe, and believe me, I know how much I owe you. But look at it this way, I'm not going anywhere and neither are you and maybe at some time in the future, maybe even next year, some project will come along, perhaps a script from one of your new books and I'll be yours, on an Aussie's word of honor."

He smiles and raises his beer glass and extends it over the table. I shake my head and smile. What else can I do? We clink glasses like the couple of mates that we are.

I arrive home a little after four o'clock. Bunny meets me at the door. She's taken the afternoon off. I had seriously considered downing a healthy snootful of Johnnie Walker at the neighborhood tavern before presenting myself but I didn't because the last thing Bunny needs, now four years sober, is a drunken husband to tend to.

"Jerry Kaplan called," she tells me as take off my jacket and toss it on the sofa.

"I'll bet he did," I say.

"He wants you to call him."

"No doubt."

"Joe, what is it? What's the matter?"

"We've lost Rod."

"Oh, Joe—"

"One of those things, Bunny. I'll survive. I'll be in the den."

I go into the den and sit behind the desk, then dial Jerry.

"It's me," I say as he comes on the line.

"Don't tell me, Joe. I already know. Rod's manager laid it out for me an hour ago and it's legit."

"I was sure it was," I say. "So what now, my friend? Do we scrap everything and wait for a sunny day?"

"No, we plow ahead, Joe. We have a budget, we have sufficient financing, we have talented director who shoots fast, we have Piper Laurie and we have Eddie Robinson."

"We don't have a Walt," I remind him.

"We have one if you want him,. His manager's been after me for weeks to give the guy a look just in case."

"Who? I ask.

He tells me. I've even seen his work. He's a pretty good actor but he's stuck in a so-so TV western series that's about to go bellyup."

"Nobody knows who he is," I say.

"The teenyboppers know him, Joe. So do a lot of grownups. Two years ago he played Biff in that TV version of 'Salesman' with Van Heflin."

"That was him?"

"That was him," Jerry says.

I hesitate, then say, "No, we need a bigger name. Find someone else. If it takes more money, I'll kick in."

"Joe—"

"Do it, Jerry. If we get it wrong, there are no do-overs and I've been waiting too long to see this screenplay get made. When you get a brainstorm, call me."

I hang up and lean back in my chair, instantly sorry that I must have sounded rude. But what the hell, I haven't come this far to get it wrong and didn't Jerry just tell me that I'm now a producer?

Bunny appears in the doorway.

"Well?"

"He had a backup in his pocket just in case."

"Really? Who?"

"What's the difference? He's unacceptable."

"I asked who," Bunny says, annoyed. I tell her. "The cowboy," she says.

"That's right. The cowboy. The TV cowboy."

"I like him. He's good."

"He's nobody."

Bunny approaches the desk and leans toward me.

"I have three words for you, sugarlips," she says.

"And what are they?"

"Garner. McQueen. Eastwood."

I stare at her. I'd been ready to exile her to the kitchen to start my supper but now the words don't come. I grab the phone and dial a number. Jerry answers.

"All right, sign the son of a bitch and then let's go out and make this Goddamned movie."

THE END

# AUTHOR'S NOTE

To the best of my knowledge, Rod Taylor was never suspected of murder and certainly not the murder of Amanda Broome, a totally fictional character. In fact he may never have received so much as a traffic ticket. I never met Mr. Taylor although I had hired him during my Universal days to appear in a pilot that I had written with the aid of my unofficial partners, Dick Levinson and Bill Link. Rod was to play a charming but ruthless crime boss, a perfect adversary for our star. When it turned out that our star was an egotistical bully with absurd ideas, no taste and an inflated sense of his own power, the three of us bowed out before filming began and left the mess for others to clean up. Too bad. I had been looking forward to getting to know Rod who went on to a long and varied career culminating in his last (cameo) role as Winston Churchill in 'Inglorious Basterds'. The pilot was made, never sold and has disappeared from view. Its sole claim to fame was providing Sean Penn with a small role that enabled him to join the Screen Actors Guild. Tippi Hedren, despite her troubles with Hitchcock, went on to make another film with him ( 'Marnie'), not a great success even with a co-star like Sean Connery. 'The Birds' was a successful film, grossing $11.4 million on a budget of $2.4 million. Reviews were mostly favorable and a majority of critics agreed that Hitchcock had done it again. The American Film Institute has named it the seventh greatest film thriller and Bravo has listed it as having one of filmdom's top 100 Scariest Movie Moments. So much for 'meaningful'. Evan Hunter's prediction proved prescient. The final scene was not a drive away with birds pecking and slashing at the canvas top of Taylor's convertible, but instead a slow walk to the car while the birds sat everywhere, quiet and immobile, watching them go. A flat finale when compared to what had gone before. Aside from the real life people involved in the filming of 'The Birds', the remaining characters are all fictional and resemblance to real people is coincidental and unintended.

# ABOUT THE AUTHOR

**Peter S. Fischer** is a former television writer-producer who currently lives in the Monterey Bay area of Central California. He is a co-creator of "Murder, She Wrote" for which he wrote over 40 scripts. Among his other credits are a dozen "Columbo" episodes and a season helming "Ellery  Queen." He has also written and produced several TV mini-series and Movies of the Week. In 1985 he was awarded an Edgar by the Mystery Writers of America. In addition to four EMMY nominations, two Golden Globe Awards for Best TV series, and an Anthony Award from the Boucheron, he has received the IBPA award for the Best Mystery Novel of the Year, a Bronze Medal from the Independent Publishers Association and an Honorable Mention from the San Francisco Festival for his first novel.

Available at Amazon.com

www.petersfischer.com

# PRAISE FOR THE HOLLYWOOD MURDER MYSTERIES

## Jezebel in Blue Satin

*In this stylish homage to the detective novels of Hollywood's Golden Age, a press agent stumbles across a starlet's dead body and into the seamy world of scheming players and morally bankrupt movie moguls.....An enjoyable fast-paced whodunit from opening act to final curtain.*

### —Kirkus Reviews

*Fans of golden era Hollywood, snappy patter and Raymond Chandler will find much to like in Peter Fischer's murder mystery series, all centered on old school studio flak, Joe Bernardi, a happy-go-lucky war veteran who finds himself immersed in tough situations.....The series fills a niche that's been superseded by explosions and violence in too much of popular culture and even though jt's a world where men are men and women are dames, its glimpses at an era where the facade of glamour and sophistication hid an uglier truth are still fun to revisit.*

### —2012 San Francisco Book Festival, Honorable Mention

*Jezebel in Blue Satin, set in 1947, finds movie studio publicist Joe Bernardi slumming it at a third rate motion picture house running on large egos and little talent. When the ingenue from the film referenced in the title winds up dead, can Joe uncover the killer before he loses his own life? Fischer makes an effortless transition from TV mystery to page turner, breathing new life into the film noir hard boiled detective tropes. Although not a professional sleuth, Joe's evolution from everyman into amateur private eye makes sense; any bad publicity can cost him his job so he has to get to the bottom of things.*

### —ForeWord Review

# We Don't Need No Stinking Badges

*A thrilling mystery packed with Hollywood glamour, intrigue and murder, set in 1948 Mexico.....Although the story features many famous faces (Humphrey Bogart, director John Huston, actor Walter Huston and novelist B. Traven, to name a few), the plot smartly focuses on those behind the scenes. The big names aren't used as gimmicks—they're merely planets for the story to rotate around. Joe Bernardi is the star of the show and this fictional tale in a real life setting (the actual set of 'Treasure of the Sierra Madre' was also fraught with problems) works well in Fischer's sure hands....A smart clever Mexican mystery.*

　　**—Kirkus Reviews**

*A former TV writer continues his old-time Hollywood mystery series, seamlessly interweaving fact and fiction in this drama that goes beyond the genre's cliches. "We Don't Need No Stinking Badges" again transports readers to post WWII Tinseltown inhabited by cinema publicist Joe Bernardi... Strong characterization propels this book. Toward the end the crosses and double-crosses become confusing, as seemingly inconsequential things such as a dead woman who was only mentioned in passing in the beginning now become matters on which the whole plot turns (but) such minor hiccups should not deter mystery lovers, Hollywood buffs or anyone who adores a good yarn.*

　　**—ForeWord Review**

*Peter S. Fischer has done it again—he has put me in a time machine and landed me in 1948. He has written a fast paced murder mystery that will have you up into the wee hours reading. If you love old movies, then this is the book for you.*

　　**—My Shelf. Com**

*This is a complex, well-crafted whodunit all on its own. There's plenty of action and adventure woven around the mystery and the characters are fully fashioned. The addition of the period piece of the 1940's filmmaking and the inclusion of big name stars as supporting characters is the whipped cream and cherry on top. It all comes together to make an engaging and fun read.*

　　**—Nyssa, Amazon Customer Review**

## Love Has Nothing to Do With It

*Fischer's experience shows in 'Love Has Nothing To Do With It', an homage to film noir and the hard-boiled detective novel. The story is complicated... but Fischer never loses the thread. The story is intricate enough to be intriguing but not baffling....Joe Bernardi's swagger is authentic and entertaining. Overall he is a likable sleuth with the dogged determination to uncover the truth.... While the outcome of the murder is an unknown until the final pages of the current title, we do know that Joe Bernardi will survive at least until 1950, when further adventures await him in the forthcoming 'Everybody Wants an Oscar'.*

**—Clarion Review**

*A stylized, suspenseful Hollywood whodunit set in 1949....Goes down smooth for murder-mystery fans and Old Hollywood junkies.*

**—Kirkus Review**

*The Hollywood Murder Mysteries just might make a great Hallmark series. Let's give this book: The envelope please: FIVE GOLDEN OSCARS.*

**—Samfreene, Amazon Customer Review**

*The writing is fantastic and, for me, the topic was a true escape into our past entertainment world. Expect it to be quite different from today's! But that's why readers will enjoy visiting Hollywood as it was in the past. A marvelous concept that hopefully will continue up into the 60s and beyond. Loved it!*

**—GABixlerReviews**

## The Unkindness of Strangers

*Winner of the Benjamin Franklin Award
for Best Mystery Book of 2012
by the Independent Book Publisher's Association.*

## Book One—1947
## JEZEBEL IN BLUE SATIN

WWII is over and Joe Bernardi has just returned home after three years as a war correspondent in Europe. Married in the heat of passion three weeks before he shipped out, he has come home to find his wife Lydia a complete stranger. It's not long before Lydia is off to Reno for a quickie divorce which Joe won't accept. Meanwhile he's been hired as a publicist by third rate movie studio, Continental Pictures. One night he enters a darkened sound stage only to discover the dead body of ambitious, would-be actress Maggie Baumann. When the police investigate, they immediately zero in on Joe as the perp. Short on evidence they attempt to frame him and almost succeed. Who really killed Maggie? Was it the over-the-hill actress trying for a comeback? Or the talentless director with delusions of grandeur? Or maybe it was the hapless leading man whose career is headed nowhere now that the "real stars" are coming back from the war. There is no shortage of suspects as the story speeds along to its exciting and unexpected conclusion.

## Book Two—1948
## WE DON'T NEED NO STINKING BADGES

Joe Bernardi is the new guy in Warner Brothers' Press Department so it's no surprise when Joe is given the unenviable task of flying to Tampico, Mexico, to bail Humphrey Bogart out of jail without the world learning about it. When he arrives he discovers that Bogie isn't the problem. So-called accidents are occurring daily on the set, slowing down the filming of "The Treasure of the Sierra Madre" and putting tempers on edge. Everyone knows who's behind the sabotage. It's the local Jefe who has a finger in every illegal pie. But suddenly the intrigue widens and the murder of one of the actors throws the company into turmoil. Day by day, Joe finds himself drawn into a dangerous web of deceit, dupliciity and blackmail that nearly costs him his life.

## Book Three–1949
## LOVE HAS NOTHING TO DO WITH IT

Joe Bernardi's ex-wife Lydia is in big, big trouble. On a Sunday evening around midnight she is seen running from the plush offices of her one- time lover, Tyler Banks. She disappears into the night leaving Banks behind, dead on the carpet with a bullet in his head. Convinced that she is innocent, Joe enlists the help of his pal, lawyer Ray Giordano, and bail bondsman Mick Clausen, to prove Lydia's innocence, even as his assignment to publicize Jimmy Cagney's comeback movie for Warner's threatens to take up all of his time. Who really pulled the trigger that night? Was it the millionaire whose influence reached into City Hall? Or the not so grieving widow finally freed from a loveless marriage. Maybe it was the partner who wanted the business all to himself as well as the new widow. And what about the mysterious envelope, the one that disappeared and everyone claims never existed? Is it the key to the killer's identity and what is the secret that has been kept hidden for the past forty years?

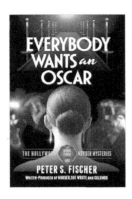

## Book Four—1950
## EVERYBODY WANTS AN OSCAR

After six long years Joe Bernardi's novel is at last finished and has been shipped to a publisher. But even as he awaits news, fingers crossed for luck, things are heating up at the studio. Soon production will begin on Tennessee Williams' "The Glass Menagerie" and Jane Wyman has her sights set on a second consecutive Academy Award. Jack Warner has just signed Gertrude Lawrence for the pivotal role of Amanda and is positive that the Oscar will go to Gertie. And meanwhile Eleanor Parker, who has gotten rave reviews for a prison picture called "Caged" is sure that 1950 is her year to take home the trophy. Faced with three very talented ladies all vying for his best efforts, Joe is resigned to performing a monumental juggling act. Thank God he has nothing else to worry about or at least that was the case until his agent informed him that a screenplay is floating around Hollywood that is a dead ringer for his newly completed novel. Will the ladies be forced to take a back seat as Joe goes after the thief that has stolen his work, his good name and six years of his life?

## Book Five—1951
## THE UNKINDNESS OF STRANGERS

Warner Brothers is getting it from all sides and Joe Bernardi seems to be everybody's favorite target. "A Streetcar Named Desire" is unproducible, they say. Too violent, too seedy, too sexy, too controversial and what's worse, it's being directed by that well-known pinko, Elia Kazan. To make matters worse, the country's number one hate monger, newspaper columnist Bryce Tremayne, is coming after Kazan with a vengeance and nothing Joe can do or say will stop him. A vicious expose column is set to run in every Hearst paper in the nation on the upcoming Sunday but a funny thing happens Friday night. Tremayne is found in a compromising condition behind the wheel of his car, a bullet hole between his eyes. Come Sunday and the scurrilous attack on Kazan does not appear. Rumors fly. Kazan is suspected but he's not the only one with a motive. Consider:

Elvira Tremayne, the unloved widow. Did Tremayne slug her one time too many?

Hubbell Cox, the flunky whose homosexuality made him a target of derision.

Willie Babbitt, the muscle. He does what he's told and what he's told to do is often unpleasant.

Jenny Coughlin, Tremayne's private secretary. But how private and what was her secret agenda?

Jed Tompkins, Elvira's father, a rich Texas cattle baron who had only contempt for his son-in-law.

Boyd Larabee, the bookkeeper, hired by Tompkins to win Cox's confidence and report back anything he's learned.

Annie Petrakis, studio makeup artist. Tremayne destroyed her lover. Has she returned the favor?

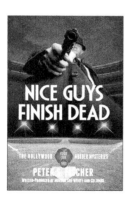

## Book Six—1952
## NICE GUYS FINISH DEAD

Ned Sharkey is a fugitive from mob revenge. For six years he's been successfully hiding out in the Los Angeles area while a $100, 000 contract for his demise hangs over his head. But when Warner Brothers begins filming "The Winning Team", the story of Grover Cleveland Alexander, Ned can't resist showing up at the ballpark to reunite with his old pals from the Chicago Cubs of the early 40's who have cameo roles in the film. Big mistake. When Joe Bernardi, Warner Brothers publicity guy, inadvertently sends a press release and a photo of Ned to the Chicago papers, mysterious people from the Windy City suddenly appear and a day later at break of dawn, Ned's body is found sprawled atop the pitcher's mound. It appears that someone is a hundred thousand dollars richer. Or maybe not. Who is the 22 year old kid posing as a 50 year old former hockey star? And what about Gordo Gagliano, a mountain of a man, who is out to find Ned no matter who he has to hurt to succeed? And why did baggy pants comic Fats McCoy jump Ned and try to kill him in the pool parlor? It sure wasn't about money. Joe , riddled with guilt because the photo he sent to the newspapers may have led to Ned's death, finds himself embroiled in a dangerous game of who-dun-it that leads from L. A. 's Wrigley Field to an upscale sports bar in Altadena to the posh mansions of Pasadena and finally to the swank clubhouse of Santa Anita racetrack.

## Book Seven—1953
## PRAY FOR US SINNERS

Joe finds himself in Quebec but it's no vacation. Alfred Hitchcock is shooting a suspenseful thriller called "I Confess" and Montgomery Clift is playing a priest accused of murder. A marriage made in heaven? Hardly. They have been at loggerheads since Day One and to make matters worse their feud is spilling out into the newspapers. When vivacious Jeanne d'Arcy, the director of the Quebec Film Commisssion volunteers to help calm the troubled waters, Joe thinks his troubles are over but that was before Jeanne got into a violent spat with a former lover and suddenly found herself under arrest on a charge of first degree murder. Guilty or not guilty? Half the clues say she did it, the other half say she is being brilliantly framed. But by who? Fingers point to the crooked Gonsalvo brothers who have ties to the Buffalo mafia family and when Joe gets too close to the truth, someone tries to shut him up. . . permanently. With the Archbishop threatening to shut down the production in the wake of the scandal, Joe finds himself torn between two loyalties.

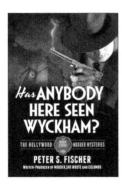

### Book Eight–1954
### HAS ANYBODY HERE SEEN WYCKHAM?

Everything was going smoothly on the set of "The High and the Mighty" until the cast and crew returned from lunch. With one exception. Wiley Wyckham, the bit player sitting in seat 24A on the airliner mockup, is among the missing, and without Wyckham sitting in place, director William Wellman cannot continue filming. A studio wide search is instituted. No Wyckham. A lookalike is hired that night, filming resumes the next day and still no Wyckham. Except that by this time, it's been discovered that Wyckham, a British actor, isn't really Wyckham at all but an imposter who may very well be an agent for the Russian government, The local police call in the FBI. The FBI calls in British counterintelligence. A manhunt for the missing actor ensues and Joe Bernardi, the picture's publicist, is right in the middle of the intrigue. Everyone's upset, especially John Wayne who is furious to learn that a possible Commie spy has been working in a picture he's producing and starring in. And then they find him . It's the dead of night on the Warner Brothers backlot and Wyckham is discovered hanging by his feet from a streetlamp, his body bloodied and tortured and very much dead. and pinned to his shirt is a piece of paper with the inscription "Sic Semper Proditor". (Thus to all traitors). Who was this man who had been posing as an obscure British actor? How did he smuggle himself into the country and what has he been up to? Has he been blackmailing an important higher-up in the film business and did the victim suddenly turn on him? Is the MI6 agent from London really who he says he is and what about the reporter from the London Daily Mail who seems to know all the right questions to ask as well all the right answers.

## Book Nine—1955
## EYEWITNESS TO MURDER

Go to New York? Not on your life. It's a lousy idea for a movie. A two year old black and white television drama? It hasn't got a prayer. This is the age of CinemaScope and VistaVision and stereophonic sound and yes, even 3-D. Burt Lancaster and Harold Hecht must be out of their minds to think they can make a hit movie out of "Marty". But then Joe Bernardi gets word that the love of his life, Bunny Lesher, is in New York and in trouble and so Joe changes his mind. He flies east to talk with the movie company and also to find Bunny and dig her out of whatever jam she's in. He finds that "Marty" is doing just fine but Bunny's jam is a lot bigger than he bargained for. She's being held by the police as an eyewitness to a brutal murder of a close friend in a lower Manhattan police station. Only a jammed pistol saved Bunny from being the killer's second victim and now she's in mortal danger because she knows what the man looks like and he's dead set on shutting her up. Permanently. Crooked lawyers, sleazy con artists and scheming businessmen cross Joe's path, determined to keep him from the truth and when the trail leads to the sports car racing circuit at Lime Rock in Connecticut, it's Joe who becomes the killer's prime target.

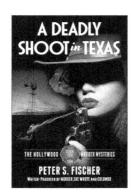

## Book Ten—1956
## A DEADLY SHOOT IN TEXAS

Joe Bernardi's in Marfa, Texas, and he's not happy. The tarantulas are big enough to carry off the cattle , the wind's strong enough to blow Marfa into New Mexico, and the temperature would make the Congo seem chilly. A few miles out of town Warner Brothers is shooting Edna Ferber's "Giant" with a cast that includes Rock Hudson, Elizabeth Taylor and James Dean and Jack Warner is paying through the nose for Joe's expertise as a publicist. After two days in Marfa Joe finds himself in a lonely cantina around midnight, tossing back a few cold ones, and being seduced by a gorgeous student young enough to be his daughter. The flirtation goes nowhere but the next morning little Miss Coed is found dead . And there's a problem. The coroner says she died between eight and nine o'clock. Not so fast, says Joe, who saw her alive as late as one a.m. When he points this out to the County Sheriff, all hell breaks loose and Joe becomes the target of some pretty ornery people. Like the Coroner and the Sheriff as well as the most powerful rancher in the county, his arrogant no-good son and his two flunkies, a crooked lawyer and a grieving father looking for justice or revenge, either one will do. Will Joe expose the murderer before the murderer turns Joe into Texas road kill? Tune in.

## Book Eleven—1957
## EVERYBODY LET'S ROCK

Big trouble is threatening the career of one of the country's hottest new teen idols and Joe Bernardi has been tapped to get to the bottom of it. Call it blackmail or call it extortion, a young woman claims that a nineteen year old Elvis Presley impregnated her and then helped arrange an abortion. There's a letter and a photo to back up her claim. Nonsense, says Colonel Tom Parker, Elvis's manager and mentor. It's a damned lie. Joe is not so sure but Parker is adamant. The accusation is a totally bogus and somebody's got to prove it. But no police can be involved and no lawyers. Just a whiff of scandal and the young man's future will be destroyed, even though he's in the midst of filming a movie that could turn him into a bona fide film star. Joe heads off to Memphis under the guise of promoting Elvis's new film and finds himself mired in a web of deceit and danger. Trusted by no one he searches in vain for the woman behind the letter, crossing paths with Sam Philips of Sun Records, a vindictive alcoholic newspaper reporter, a disgraced doctor with a seedy past, and a desperate con artist determined to keep Joe from learning the truth.

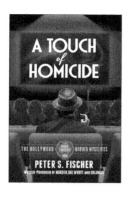

## Book Twelve—1958
## A TOUCH OF HOMICIDE

It takes a lot to impress Joe Bernardi. He likes his job and the people he deals with but nobody is really special. Nobody, that is, except for Orson Welles, and when Avery Sterling, a bottom feeding excuse for a producer, asks Joe's help in saving Welles from an industry-wide smear campaign, Joe jumps in, heedless that the pool he has just plunged into is as dry as a vermouthless martini. A couple of days later, Sterling is found dead in his office and the police immediately zero in on two suspects—Joe who has an alibi and Welles who does not. Not to worry, there are plenty of clues at the crime scene including a blood stained monogrammed handkerchief, a rejected screenplay, a pair of black-rimmed reading glasses, a distinctive gold earring and petals from a white carnation. What's more, no less than four people threatened to kill him in front of witnesses. A case so simple a two-year old could solve it but the cop on the case is a dimwit whose uncle is on the staff of the police commissioner. Will Joe and Orson solve the case before one of them gets arrested for murder? Will an out-of-town hitman kill one or both of them? Worst of all, will Orson leave town leaving Joe holding the proverbial bag?

## Book Thirteen—1959
## SOME LIKE 'EM DEAD

After thirteen years, the great chase is over and Joe Bernardi is marrying Bunny Lesher. After a brief weekend honeymoon, it'll be back to work for them both; Bunny at the Valley News where she has just been named Assistant Editor and Joe publicizing Billy Wilder's new movie, Some Like It Hot about two musicians hiding out from the mob in an all-girl band. It boasts a great script and a stellar cast that includes Tony Curtis, Jack Lemmon and Marilyn Monroe, so what could go wrong? Plenty and it starts with Shirley Davenport, Bunny's protege at the News, who has been assigned to the entertainment pages. To placate Bunny and against his better judgement Joe gives Shirley a press credential for the shoot and from the start, she is a destructive force, alienating cast and crew, including Billy Wilder, who does not suffer fools easily. Someone must have become really fed up with her because one misty morning a few hundred yards down the beach from the famed Hotel Del Coronado, Shirley's lifeless body, her head bashed in with a blunt instrument, is discovered by joggers. This after she'd been seen lunching with George Raft; hobnobbing with up and coming actor, Vic Steele; angrily ignoring fellow journalist Hank Kendall; exchanging jealous looks with hair stylist Evie MacPherson; and making a general nuisance of herself everywhere she turned. United Artists is aghast and so is Joe This murder has to be solved and removed from the front pages of America's newspapers as soon as possible or when it's released, this picture will be known as 'the murder movie', hardly a selling point for a rollicking comedy.

## Book Fourteen—1960
## DEAD MEN PAY NO DEBTS

Among the hard and fast rules in Joe Bernardi's life is this one:
Do not, under any circumstances, travel east during the winter months. In this way one avoids dealing with snow, ice, sleet, frostbite and pneumonia. Unfortunately he has had to break this rule and having done so, is paying the price. His novel 'A Family of Strangers' has been optioned for a major motion picture and he needs to fly east in January to meet with the talented director who has taken the option. Stuart Rosenberg, in the midst of directing "Murder Inc." an expose of the 1930's gang of killers for hire, has insisted Joe write the screenplay and he needs several days to guide Joe in the right direction. Reluctantly Joe agrees, a decision which he will quickly rue when he finds himself up to his belly button with drug dealers, loan sharks, Mafia hit men, wannabe Broadway stars and an up and coming New York actor named Peter Falk who may be on the verge of stardom. Someone has beaten drug dealer Gino Finucci to death and left his body in the basement of The Mudhole, an off-off-Broadway theater which is home to Amythyst Breen, a one time darling of Broadway struggling to find her way back to the top and also Jonathan Harker, slimy and ambitious, an actor caught in the grip of drug addiction even as he struggles to get that one lucky break that will propel him to stardom. Even as Joe fights to remain above the fray, he can feel himself being inexorably drawn into the intrigue of underworld vendettas culminating in a face to face confrontation with Carlo Gambino, the boss of bosses, and the most powerful Mafia chieftain in New York City.

## Book Fifteen—1961
## APPLE ANNIE AND THE DUDE

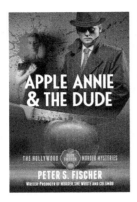

Joe Bernardi is a sucker for a sad story and especially when it comes from an old pal like Lila James who, after years of trying, has landed a plum assignment as a movie publicist. Frank Capra has okayed her for his newest film, A Pocketful of Miracles, now shooting on the Paramount lot. Get this right and her little company has a big future which is when God intervenes by inflicting her with a broken leg which will put her out of commission for at least a couple of weeks. Enter Joe as Sir Galahad to save the day and fill in. A simple favor, you say? Not so fast. First he'll have to deal with Heather Leeds, Lila's assistant, an ambitious tart in the mold of Eve Harrington, a devious cupcake who makes enemies the way Betty Crocker makes biscuits. Making his job even more difficult are the on-set feuds between Bette Davis and Glenn Ford with Capra getting migraines trying to referee. And then the fun really starts as a mysterious woman named Claire Philby from Northwestern University shows up to give Heather an award and maybe something else she never bargained for. Who killed Heather Leeds? Was it Philby or maybe Heather's husband Buddy Lovejoy, a struggling television writer, or perhaps even his writing partner, Seth Donnelley. And what about Heather's ex-husband Travis Wright who was just released from prison and claims Heather owes him $9,000,000 which he left in her care? Of more concern to Joe is the shadow of suspicion that has fallen on Dexter Craven, an old friend from the Warner Bros. days. Good old Lila, she's lying peacefully in a hospital bed while Joe deals with a nest of vipers, one of which is a cold blooded killer, and a movie in the making which is being tattered by conflicting egos. It's enough to make a man long for happier days when he was slogging through muddy France at the tail-end of World War II.

## Book Sixteen—1962
## 'TILL DEATH US DO PART

Who would want to kill a sweet old guy like Mike O'Malley, the prop master on Universal's "To Kill a Mockingbird"? Nobody, but dead he is, the victim of a hit and run that looks more like deliberate murder than accidental death. More likely the killer was after Mike's grandson Rory who had earned the enmity of Hank Greb, a burly mean-spirited teamster as well as Wayne Daniels, a wannabe actor, who claims erroneously that Rory's carelessness caused his face to be disfigured. Is this any of Joe Bernardi's business? Not really but when he showed up on the Mockingbird set as a favor to his hospitalized partner, Bertha Bowles, to woo newcomer William Windom to join the Bowles & Bernardi management firm, Joe was sucked into the situation right up to his tonsils, something he had little time for since his first priority was handling publicity for 'Lilies of the Field', a Sidney Poitier film, shooting in Tucson. Meanwhile Joe, who longs to write a second novel, has become increasingly bored with working at movie promotion and publicity. A twist of fate finds him befriended by Truman Capote and by Harper Lee who, like Joe, is trying to find that elusive second novel. Both are huge admirers of Joe's highly praised first novel and vow to help Joe get it made as a motion picture, even as Joe tries to expose the truth about Mike O'Malleys' death.

## Book Seventeen—1963
## CUE THE CROWS

How do you make a movie when the star of your dreams, eager to sign, is suddenly faced with a murder charge and could spend the rest of his life cooped up in San Quentin? Joe Bernardi, author, screenwriter and possibly a co-producer, has traveled north along the California coastline to Bodega Bay to hobnob with Rod Taylor who is filming Alfred Hitchcock's thriller, 'The Birds'. Rod is on the verge of signing the contract when a funny thing happens. The body of a young attractive redhead named Amanda Broome is found dead in the trunk of his Corvette. Taylor screams frame-up, even though Amanda has been stalking him for weeks and they had a violent and very public argument only hours before her body was discovered. Further filming of 'The Birds' is in jeopardy and so is the filming of Joe's movie based on his best-selling book. Looming large in the midst of this is Henrietta Boyle, a county attorney with gubernatorial ambitions and what better way to grease the path to the State House than to convict a famous movie star of homicide. But who else might have an interest in seeing Amanda dead? Perhaps her aunt, executrix of a trust fund which would have made Amanda a millionairess in a few short weeks. A definite possibility . Determined to prove Taylor innocent, Joe follows a trail that leads from a teen hangout in Palo Alto to the halls of academia to a posh country club where a triple A credit rating is the first requirement for membership. When a mysterious car tries to run Joe off the road into a deep and deadly crevasse in the hills above the Bay, he knows he's getting close to the truth but will the truth be revealed before Joe becomes buzzard bait?

Made in the USA
Middletown, DE
15 August 2021

46135132R00126